Shop Front

Samuel Best

Published by Fledgling Press 2014

www.fledglingpress.co.uk

Cover design: Michael O'Shea
www.michaeloshea.co.uk

Printed and bound by:
Bell & Bain Limited, Glasgow

ISBN 9781905916726

To Charlene, always.

Acknowledgements

To Clare Cain, Michael O'Shea and Fledgling Press.

To Craig Lamont, for dreaming big with me.

To Dickson Telfer, for sharpening every sentence.

To Allan Wilson, let's start a retail-lit scene!

To Alan Bissett, for inspiring me.

To Doug Johnstone, for encouraging me.

To Rodge Glass, for teaching me.

To Ruby and Daisy, for their vocal input.

To Ted, for his unwavering support.

Charlene, from the first to the last word, you've been there. Thank you for everything.

1

The doors clunk shut behind me. I look around the train for a seat but there are none free. People sit squashed up against each other, trying to read books or text. I stand in the middle of the carriage, hand firmly grasping the back of someone's seat. The information bar flickers into life and scrolls place names in quick succession. The announcement repeats the locations but they're distorted and difficult to hear. I check my phone.

5:45p.m.   1 New Message.   Mum.

Hi Ben hope you are ok. are you on the train now?

I text back: Yeah, I'm fine. Just leaving now. Back in half an hour x

'The end of an era,' Dad had said, when I told him I was thinking of moving back home. 'We'd love to have you back, son. Your mum will be thrilled!'

I knew she would be.

'It'll be like you're seventeen again!' she said when she heard, her laughter bouncing down the phone line. 'Like going back in time.'

Like the past 4 years of writing essays, reading books

and lectures lectures lectures hadn't happened. I'm the same person; just older, poorer, and with BA (Hons) at the end of my name. Then I felt guilty for resenting the move home. I'm an English graduate; I should be happy to have a roof over my head.

The careers adviser had talked to me in first year. He told me an English degree was a good choice for Higher Education and that I would have many options available to me.

'Advertising, teaching, library work, journalism, creative writing, publishing, T.V. and radio work. The list goes on, Ben.'

I'd left his office with a grin on my face and a swagger in my step. Now, after graduation, it felt like a grimace and a limp. I'd searched the job websites, handed CVs into shops with signs in the windows, handed CVs into shops without signs in the windows, signed on, got told I had to 'widen my search to include non-graduate jobs', signed off; the lot. And still nothing. 'Nothingness is the yet-to-be-born god of the world,' said Büchner. He was talking about the Scottish job market, I was pretty sure.

Until one day, my mum phoned me, chattering about a new development in Linlithgow.

'It's awful. As if we need another supermarket! And to think they'll ruin that nice green field on the way into town. What will the tourists think, coming to visit the Royal Burgh and the first thing they see is a bloody Asda?'

I looked it up online. The rumours were true. Asda was wading into town, challenging Tesco and Sainsbury's to the championship. It'd be a royal rumble, only I knew which side I'd be on. After much internal debate – *Is this giving up? No, it's tiding myself over* – I handed in my CV with the best covering letter anyone's ever seen. The phone rang one evening and I just knew.

'Hello?' I answered.

'Ben Hamilton?'

They called me in for a 'quick chat' and in five minutes my life changed. Gone were the days of boredom and poverty; here was a chance for boredom and breadline existence. Dad was overjoyed. No more arguments.

'Well, Ben, you're the one who did an English degree in a recession. I told you to try for something more secure, but you insisted.'

'There are jobs for English graduates, Dad, but I'm not going to find one stacking fucking shelves for £5 an hour.'

'I am not having you turn out like some waster who stumbles about pissed out of his head at 2pm on a Saturday because you have nothing better to do. You need a job. End of.'

It's my first day tomorrow and I reckon I know exactly what to expect. The manager will be a nightmare. Either a graduate, like me, who's been forced to give up looking for jobs in the area they've trained in; or a grunt who's worked their way up. They'll give me lists of tasks that don't really matter in the grand scheme of things and expect me to pour my heart and soul into scrubbing shelves or rotating stock. I know it's snobby to look down on jobs like that now I have a degree, but there's a little part of me that's terrified this is both the start and end of the rest of my life. What if I'm one of those overqualified statistics the government use to slag universities off? This has to be temporary, I repeat to myself. Temporary.

The train judders and I grip the seat hard, saving myself from falling. A woman behind me loses her balance and crashes full force into my back. She steadies herself, mumbles an apology, and stuffs her rhubarb face back into her book. We stop. I look out the window and try to work out where we are. Some no man's land in-between Glasgow and Falkirk. Other people on the train look around, questions in their eyes. A loud ping from the PA system and the distorted voice crackles to life again.

'Ladies and gentlemen, on behalf of ScotRail, we are sorry for the delay. There has been an incident ahead of us and I will keep you informed of any further developments. Once again, ScotRail apologises for any inconvenience this delay may cause.'

The speech ends with a pop and the carriage erupts into conversation. I look at my phone again.

1 New Message. Mum.

Let us know when your at the station and ill put dinner on.

An old man in a suit standing next to me leans over. 'Any idea what's going on?'

I look at him, blank faced. 'How would I know what's happening?'

'Eh, I dunno. That thing of yours not get updates?' He points at my phone.

'This thing barely gets text messages,' I say, waving the old brick at him.

He shrugs and turns around, asking someone else if they know anything. I wonder about the possibilities. Terrorists storming trains, taking hostages, robbing and murdering people. Or someone sitting quietly with a rucksack of wires and a ticking clock. I wait for the lights to cut out, for people to scream, for gruff voices to order us onto the ground. But nothing happens. Then *ping*.

'Ladies and gentlemen, ScotRail would like to apologise for the delay. We are still awaiting news of the disruption and I will update you as soon as we know anything. Uh, once again, ScotRail apologises for any inconvenience this may cause.'

There's a crackle but the PA is still on. 'No idea, mate. Wish control would fucking tell us something instead of making us sit around and wait. Dickheads.'

Everyone laughs. I imagine the newspapers tomorrow, probably The Sun or Daily Mail. TRAIN TANNOY SWEARING SHAME. The article would be light, bashed out in under five minutes, but the comments would be outraged that 'there were kids on board and thats not acceptible' and probably go on to blame the entire public sector.

People on phones tell girlfriends, wives, husbands, babysitters, that they're going to be late and they're sorry. Some coo I love yous and kisses, others mutter 'Well it's not my bloody fault is it?' I look at my phone again. 6:20pm. I should be in Linlithgow by now. The screen flashes.

1 New Message. Mum.

Are you okay? not heard from you.

I text her back a quick explanation. Train's delayed. Will let you know when we're moving again.

The train judders and jolts into motion, slowly. Everyone's looking around, grateful that we're not stranded in the middle of nowhere anymore. As the conversation subsides and people turn back to their laptops, phones or books, there's another *ping*.

'Ladies and gentlemen, as you will see we are on the move again. ScotRail would like to again apologise for the delay. This was caused by an accident at Linlithgow station, which remains closed. As such, this train will now terminate at Polmont station and a replacement bus service will take over the remainder of your journey.'

The train is silent for a moment and then bursts back into life. Gesturing, shouting, kicking anger fills the carriage. 'Polmont? POLMONT? They're dumping us in fucking Polmont?!'

I text Mum again. Train terminating at Polmont. Come get me?

Over the commotion, the PA announces Falkirk High and the doors hiss open. The carriage clears a little and I find a seat. After watching housing estates fly past for a minute, I flick through my phonebook, just for something to do.

Adam
Alistair
Amy
Ashley

Last I'd heard, Adam did admin for a computer games company; Alistair was still studying to become an accountant; Amy had started her own business and Ashley was doing filing in a lawyer's office. Tomorrow I'm officially a sales assistant. What decision was it that led to this? Why was it me who ended up in an irrelevant job, not one of them? At what point did things for me change? Maybe it was studying English, like Dad said. Maybe it was my choice of uni. Maybe having a degree didn't really matter after all. My eyes flick back into focus and I look at the information bar. The next stop is Polmont.

I look outside and see that it's raining. Mum hasn't texted back and my jacket doesn't have a hood. The train slows and eventually stops. Doors judder open, letting the weather spill into the carriage. I get up and step out, holding a Metro over my head. I run to the shelter but it's locked and the windows have been boarded up. *Bloody vandals*, Dad would say.

I squint left and right, looking for Mum or the car's headlights, but the station is empty and dark. A crisp packet blows up in the wind and hurtles past me onto the tracks as I watch a crow try to fly against the wind. I keep checking my phone, starting to worry that the rain might seep through the gaps and break it. As I go to put it away, the screen lights up and I press Read.

In the car park now.

I run over, my face burning with the cold and the rain, and see the car waiting. Mum starts the engine and the headlights flash on. In the downpour they look like they are crying or melting. I open the door and slide into the passenger seat.

'Hiya!' Mum coos. 'How are you? Soaking?'

'Yeah, pure drenched,' I say, fastening my seatbelt.

'Pure, eh? Won't find much of that West Coast talk back in Linlithgow, I'm afraid. You'll have to settle into the Central accent now.' She looks outside and pulls a face, tucking her brown waves behind her ears. 'God, what a night.'

We sit in silence for a bit as she pulls back onto the main road. I adjust the heating.

'Take it you heard about the station?' she asks.

'I heard there was an accident but that's it.'

'Suicide,' she says, the word hanging in the air. 'The whole station's cordoned off but I stopped and asked a policeman. Some poor guy jumped in front of a train, apparently. They've been finding bits of him all over the car park.'

I stare out of the window and watch as the sky gets darker.

'Not the first time that's happened either,' she says.

We sit quietly for a little while longer and then she changes the subject.

'So, are you excited about moving back?'

'About as excited as I can be, yeah.'

'Get to see all your old friends and everything,' she smiles, trying to make this seem better.

'All my old friends moved away, Mum. Uni, jobs, families.'

She shrugs slightly, eyes fixed on the road. We don't talk much for the rest of the journey.

Pulling up, I thank Mum for the lift. She collects her handbag from the back seat as I step out, my jacket over my head since the Metro got soaked through. I glance up at the house. My parents' house. My home now. Again. On a sunny day it would look picturesque but everything looks depressing in the rain. We both run into the house, our footsteps splashing on the path.

Inside, Dad's had the heating on, and I can hear the TV in the sitting room. An audience applauding. It feels almost like a welcome party. I hang my jacket to dry and take off my shoes as Mum motions me through. I step into the living room and Dad mutes his show. He stands up and shakes my hand, smiling. He's getting a bit of a stomach and his hair's beginning to thin, but his beard is as full as ever.

'Ben! How are you? Not too wet, I hope.'

'I'm alright, Dad, thanks. Just a spot of bother with the trains.'

'Yes, your mother mentioned. What was it this time? Broken down again?'

'Suicide,' I say. The air seems to chill with that word.

'Ah,' Dad looks down, frowning. 'Bit inconsiderate, don't you think? Causing all that disruption...'

I look at him for a moment, his face solid and straight, and then he cracks into a laugh.

'I'm joking! Of course, it's horrible. Come on, sit down, have a drink. *Welcome home.*'

Mum brings through three glasses and a bottle and pours the red until the glasses are 'filled properly', as she would say. To the brim is what most people would call it.

'Wine is bottled poetry,' Dad says, taking his glass from Mum. 'You know who said that?'

I pause for a moment, thinking hard. 'Stevenson?' I try.

'Ah well done – a true English student!' he laughs. 'So, tell me about this Asda job.'

2

'So you're the new lad, eh?'

'Yeah, I suppose so,' I laugh.

'Something funny about that?'

'No. Sorry.'

'Aw, I'm only jokin'. Dinnae worry yourself. I'm Paul an' I'm your manager. So you're on replen' an' service. That means you'll be putting the stock oot an' helping folk who dinnae have a clue, right?'

Paul laughs to himself as we walk up and down the aisles. He's probably in his early 30s. Old enough to be a team leader, but young enough that everyone isn't scared of him.

'Have ye done anythin' like this before?'

'Once, when I was about 15, yeah. In a pet shop for work experience with school.'

'Great stuff. So ye'll ken all aboot the importance of customer service an' aw that.'

'Yeah, 'the customer is always right'.'

'Aye ... except they're no' always right.'

'How do you mean?'

He sighs. 'See, ye'll get folk in here who think they

ken their rights, but they don't. Customers always *think* they're right but mostly they dinnae huv a leg tae stand on.'

'Right.'

'No' always! Ha ha!'

Paul's a funny guy.

'I mean, see this?' He picks up a jar of freeze-dried coffee. 'It says £2.64, but see if some auld man brings it tae the till an' I say, 'Here, that's £4 now', that means he *hus* tae pay that. None ae this 'It says on the shelf so that's what ye huv tae charge' pish. It's in the law.'

I have no idea if this is true but Paul's so sure of himself I don't dare doubt him.

'If ye ever git any bother off somewan like that, jist gie me a shout.'

'Will do.'

We keep walking and eventually come to a big set of green plastic sheets. The kind I always wanted to look behind when I was little, but was too scared. The kind that lead 'intae the back' where staff go and pretend to look for your stuff. Paul motions me through. Past them is the warehouse. Cold and grey, I imagine all warehouses must look the same.

'It's empty jist now 'cause fuck aw came in the day, but it's usually packed. Delivery comes in aboot midday, if it's on time. Normally aboot 20 pallets, plus trolleys. It'll be your job tae haul that oot an' put it on the shelves. Neatly, mind. Standards huv tae be kept up. Ye'll do that at the end ae the night. It's murder but somewan hus tae do it. Jist go round makin sure everythin's in the right place, aw neat an' lined up, an' that the floor's no' filthy.'

'Right.'

'Any questions so far?'

'No, I think I'm okay.'

'That's wit I like tae hear. So I suppose I'd better take ye tae meet the rest ae the team. You'll already ken Linda, the wan who interviewed ye. She's in the night too, on the desk, an' the rest are oot on the shop floor probably skiving like usual. Here...'

He holds the plastic open for me again and we walk back onto the shop floor. The music is a bit louder here. Pop songs, slightly out-of-date, played quietly enough that you wouldn't notice it unless you stopped and listened. Reminds me of living in halls; listening through the walls to flatmates playing 'retro' CDs from the early 2000s.

Paul walks ahead of me, still talking. I adjust the badges on my chest. One says BEN and the other says TRAINEE.

'... You listening tae me?' Paul turns round as he walks.

'Sorry, my badge ... What was it you said?'

'I wis saying I hope ye stay longer than the last boy we hud daein' your job. Fucked off tae uni in the autumn without daein' his notice, cheeky git.'

'Oh right. No worries there: I'm fresh out of uni.'

'Wit did ye do there?'

'English Lit. Bit of a waste of time, if I'm honest.'

'Aye, it sounds it.' He laughs again, that laugh. 'Right, jist roond this corner here.'

We turn a corner and see three boys leaning against a crate full of boxes. They all quickly put mobile phones back in their pockets and say 'Alright Paul?'

'I saw that, boys, but I'll pretend I didnae. This is Ben,' he motions to me. 'He'll be joining you wi' replen' an' service. Yous can show him the ropes; how tae face the stock, where it all goes, ken? Ben, this is Pete, Jake and Niall.' He points at each of the boys in turn. 'Pete an' Niall are on replen' the night, an' Jake's daein' service but he'll be chippin' in whenever it's quiet. I'll be aboot. I've git some paperwork tae do in the office but I'll come check on yous later, see how ye're gettin' on. I don't huv a proper safety knife for ye, Ben, but this'll dae for now,' Paul hands me a small red box cutter, pats me on the arm and walks off, whistling along to the music.

I look at the team. Niall's back on his phone, texting quickly. He's about six foot, slim with short, gelled brown hair. Footballer-looking. Pete's taller still, and more filled out. He looks a couple of years older than the others – a mini Paul in the making, perhaps. He and Jake are laughing at something I didn't hear. Jake looks to me and grins, adjusting a leather cuff on his wrist before smoothing out his long, black fringe. The smallest of the three, I reckon he's probably the youngest too.

'So, Ben, what do you do?' he asks.

'Uhm, well I've just finished wasting my time with uni and now I'm just trying to earn a bit of cash. Make a bit of a living, y'know?'

'You're probably in the wrong job for that then. Pay's fuck all here and no one ever gets promoted.'

Pete nods his head, scratches his stubbly beard, grabs a box and cuts it open. The knife glides through the tape. He makes it look effortless, second nature.

'Wit d'you hink ae Paul, then?' Niall asks, smiling.

'Yeah, he seems pretty sound. He's been alright with me, anyway. What about you?'

'Aw, Paul's awright. He can be harsh if ye git on his bad side but he's usually no' bad. Jist do yer work an' he willnae complain.'

'He's a good guy to get a drink with too,' Pete chips in, throwing boxes of Crunchy Nut to Jake; who catches three but drops the last one. 'Usually up for buying you a pint when you're out.'

'Ha, mind that time we all went out and that guy started on you, Pete?' Jake laughs.

'Aye, wit started aw that again?' Niall stops cutting the box he's holding and looks at Pete.

Pete sighs and turns to me. 'We were all out, the four of us, just getting a quiet drink, like. A few pints, maybe some shots. And this guy comes up to me. This huge guy comes up to me at the bar.'

'Swaggering like a dick,' says Jake.

'Yeah, swaggering, like, totally acting the big man. Polo shirt, Diesel jeans, pint in his hand. Going like, 'Here, ah ken you. You're that wee dick who jumped ma cousin last week.' But I've got no idea what he's on about. I mean, I know I'm a big guy myself, but I'm not the kinda guy who goes out jumping folk for no reason. So I'm like 'Nah, mate, that wisnae me, sorry."

'Shitein' yerself,' laughs Niall.

'Fuck off.' Pete says. There's a sharp look on his face for a second but then he goes back to his story. 'So I say, 'Nah, pal, you've got the wrong guy', and this big lad's like, 'Nah, ah ken it wis you. You battered ma cousin last week, ah ken that. So how's it funny now, when you're the wan gonnae get battered?' And then this dick' – he points at Niall – 'comes over, 'cause he was still sitting back at the table. He comes over, squares up to the guy and just goes, 'Here, mate, gonnae fuck off?"

'An' the guy disnae ken wit tae do!' Niall's laughing loudly now, leaning on the pallet truck. 'He's like, 'Wit did you say, pal? Wit ... did ... you ... say ... tae ... me?' Flexin' his muscles, fist clenched an' that, an' they're aw watchin', goin' like 'Fuckin' hell, man', an' Pete's still pissin' his jeans, all feart.'

'Was I fuck. So we're all watching Niall square up to this big guy, and the lad knows he's outnumbered 'cause he's just out with this girl, right. And she's hiding away, staying right out. Barely even saw her face, she's so tucked away. So this lad knows he's outnumbered but he's still acting like the hard man, and he goes, 'I'll knock you out, son. You an' yer team.' Drains his glass and sits it on the bar. And Niall just looks at him, pulls out this wee red thing, opens it up and goes, 'If you touch wan ae us I will cut you down tae yer fuckin' gizzards, right?"

Jake points at my hand.

'It was one of them. A wee box cutter. Niall just had it from work, he doesn't carry one all the time – I hope – but he pulls it on the guy, this bare razor in his hand.'

'An' the guy jist fuckin' legs it!' Niall laughs. 'Left his girl an' aw. We hud tae leave pretty sharp, like, after that. Cannae go back either, but it wis worth it.' Niall's acting it out, pulling his own safety knife from his pocket and holding it up at Jake. 'Made me hink I should carry wan ae these wee men aw the time.'

'Jesus,' I say. 'When was that?'

"Bout two weeks ago. Usually oot every Friday down The Arms 'til that. Now we're lookin' at The Auld Hole by the Cross. You should come themorra,' Niall says as Pete shoots Jake a look and picks up another box. He looks at the label, pulls a face, and then throws it back in the pile.

'Uhm, yeah, why not?' I say. 'If that's alright, I mean.'

'Aye, we'll put you through yer paces, make sure yer gid enough tae join the team.' Niall winks. 'Cannae work here an' no' be able tae handle yer drink, ken?'

The other boys laugh and continue to push boxes onto the shelves, packing them in tightly. I join in and we work in silence for a few minutes. The only sound is the music playing from the ceiling.

'Seen that Boy George has announced tour dates?' says Jake, 'South America. Playing in Brazil.'

'You an' your fuckin' 80s music,' Niall says, 'S'aw we ever git fae you. Drives me mad. Standin there wi' your fuckin' Duran Duran haircut, talkin' aboot Boy George. Boy. Fuckin'. George. He's a wee criminal wi' wan gid song. I was fine wi' him doin aw the drugs an' that. That's awright if ye can handle it. But lockin' that boy up wis a step too far. That an' they tattoos on his heid. Too far, man.'

'I wouldn't go see him, to be honest. He sounds like a nutter, if you ask me,' Pete says, manoeuvring the pallet on to the truck. 'Got that Karma song though. That's alright.'

'Adam Ant. That's what I'm excited about. New album out soon,' Jake continues, undeterred. 'It's been too long. I'd see him wherever he plays.'

'Aye, Adam Ant. Him an' aw,' Niall vents. 'Mind that time you turned up tae that night oot aw dressed up? Looked like something outae Bon Jovi crossed wi' Prince Charming. Wit wis it you were wearin again? Some shite...'

'Aw, was that the time he wore white boots?' asks Pete, his tone stretched.

'Aye! That's the wan,' Niall laughs as Jake turns away, red-faced. 'Fuckin' white cowboy boots, man. Wit were you thinkin'? Looked like ye were aboot tae round up the rest ae the Village People.'

'Yeah, well, they were nice boots. They really were, Ben.' Jake turns to me. 'White leather, with this really nice stitching all around them. They just didn't get what I was going for.' He nods at the other two.

'Aye, an' wit wis it you were goin' fur, exactly?' asks Niall. 'A beatin' fae some workie in the toilets?'

'It was a look inspired by Adam Ant and Bret Michaels

18

from Poison, actually. Proper glitzy old rock an' roll,' Jake glares, speaking through clenched teeth.

'Bret Michaels? Even Bret Michaels wouldnae huv been seen deid in they boots!' Niall laughs. 'Him an' Adam Ant. They'd huv been like 'Naw, that's too far. They look fuckin' daft, man.' 'Aye, Adam, ridicule *is* sumhin tae be scared of!''

'Aye, thanks. Well I'll not be wearing them again, anyway. Seventy pounds down the fucking drain. Just sitting in my wardrobe now.'

'Seventy quid?' Pete stops the truck. 'Christ, Jake, what were you thinking?!'

'I dunno. I thought they were nice.' Jake scuffs his shoe off the kick-plate at the side of the aisle and corrects a display of double chocolate cookies. 'And anyway Niall, what about that time you turned up to work with that knock-off jacket, eh? **Le Cock Sportif** printed on the front? You looked a right tool.'

'Aye, but I'd rather waste fifteen pound on a shitey jacket than seventy on fuckin' space boots. An' anyrate, at least I ken that of aw the decades no' tae try an' copy, it's the fuckin' 80s.'

'Here! Enough jabberin'!' Paul's voice shouts down the aisle. 'Yous don't git paid tae chat. Fuckin' move it!'

We all mumble sorry and walk towards the warehouse, Pete still towing the empty pallet. Jake's next to me and I see him glance in my direction. 'Still think they boots are magic.'

We push through the plastic sheets and into the

warehouse, all scuffing our shoes along the ground as we walk.

'So you're coming tomorrow then?' asks Pete, parking the pallet truck.

'Yeah, that'd be great. Cheers for the invite,' I say, catching him throwing a look at Jake again.

'Jist remember tae bring yer fightin' boots, son,' Niall says as he walks over, knife in hand.

He winks and I laugh.

3

'Welcome to university!' he'd said, his arms open wide, encompassing us all, inviting us into his world. 'This is the start of the rest of your life. A whole different world to secondary school or college, you'll find. You'll be studying your subject of choice with a group of like-minded individuals. University is where you will develop and shape who you are as a person.'

I had been terrified and excited in equal measures. Freshers' Week was easy to muddle through: no fear of the impending classes because most people couldn't even remember what classes they were taking. I hadn't been too keen on the whole 'party week' idea at first – wary of turning into one of those waster students who live in paid-for flats, don't work and yet somehow still miss all of their classes – but I'd been won over eventually. My new flatmates, Amy, Dean and Ashley, had persuaded me to come out 'just for one'. One turned into £20-worth of happy hour pints and shots and we turned into a gang of student mates.

Amy was studying business and accounting, aiming to be the next Michelle Mone.

'Except no' wi' lingerie,' she'd said. 'There's enough big tits in this world that dinnae need an extra boost.' I remembered her nodding at a group of lads downing shots and beating their chests like cavemen over a kill.

Dean was a big guy: my first impression had been wondering what steroids he took in the womb. He worked as a bouncer to earn the cash for uni and was training to be a primary school teacher. He had sighed when Amy wondered aloud if he was gay.

'That's what everyone asks. And no. Straight as they come. I just love kids and I've always wanted to go into teaching.'

Lastly there was Ashley. She was the fountain of knowledge in the flat. Any question posed would be answered with absolute confidence and absolutely right. On nights out she used her extensive knowledge to beat pub quiz machines and buy us rounds. She wanted to be a lawyer and consequently no one ever dared argue with her.

On the first day of classes, after a week of hangovers and drinks paid for by beaten puggies, we had all woken up feeling the same nervous excitement. It was finally here. We said goodbye after a hectic morning and all rushed off to our respective introductory classes. I took a seat in the middle of the English lecture hall, empty spaces either side of me. The hall had gradually filled and I realised I had never been in a room with so many people before. I looked around, amazed at the sheer number of people who had come to study English, the number of people who loved words just as much as me, possibly more so.

Eventually every seat was filled and I ended up sitting next to a flustered-looking man in his late 40s and a guy about my age, who had strutted in like Mick Jagger, all skinny jeans, teased hair and leather jacket. He sat down with a slump, folding his legs under the desk, his arms behind his head.

A tall, thin man walked in to the room and stood behind the lectern. The room had been buzzing with conversation and laughter but quickly dulled to silence. The man smiled. He did a brief welcome speech and then went on to tell us all about the wonderful world of education.

'You will be tested and you will be expected to push yourself. For some of you this can prove too much, but I want each and every one of you to know that if you are ever struggling, or have any doubts, come and see one of your tutors and we will endeavour to help you to the best of our ability. We are not here to do the work for you but we will be here if you need a helping hand.'

He paused and I looked down at my notepad. The page was still empty, my pen still sitting ready in my hand. I wasn't sure if I should be writing this down but when I looked around I noticed no one else was either.

'Now, English students, you will probably have studied a lot of Shakespeare in school. Am I right?'

The crowd murmured in agreement. The man smiled again.

'Well, you will be pleased to know that in this university we believe in studying a wide array of texts. If you have already looked at the reading list – and I hope you have – you will see that this year we will be studying from classic-era Greek plays all the way up to last year's Somerset Maugham Award winner.'

I bent down to my bag, a new satchel from T.K. Maxx (reduced by 70%, Mum said), and raked inside for the reading list. Between folders (empty), packets of pens (freshly opened) and notebooks (again, empty) I found the sheet of paper listing the required reading for Core English. I read it over, excitement bubbling through my organs.

'I've read that book,' I thought, scanning over the titles.

'I know that writer,' I thought, scanning over the names.

'This course was made for me,' I thought, my eyes returning to watch the man at the front of the hall.

He kept talking, listing how many hours a week we should put into study, how to submit the assignments (FOUR whole essays!), and what the final exam format would be like. As he talked I tapped my pen gently against my palm. After a while, the mature student to my left cleared his throat and I dropped the pen. I bent down again, looking amongst the clutter of bags and feet, but couldn't spot it. As I went to sit back up the guy next to me moved his feet slightly so he could sit with his legs spread apart, the way men do when they're asserting how manly they are because they have cocks that reach their knees and balls as big as grapefruit.

Just beside his right heel I saw a glint of plastic. I couldn't reach it, so I leaned over.

'Excuse me ... mate? Could you get my pen for me?'

He didn't reply. Didn't even turn his head. I cleared my throat and whispered a bit louder.

'Sorry, could you just–?'

The mature student shh-ed loudly and I sat back, defeated. I waited a while. A few minutes, maybe, listening to the web address for the English essay style guide (repeated in the handbook, thankfully), before I tried again. This time, I turned to my right and tapped the guy on his leather-jacketed arm. He jumped as though woken from a deep sleep and pulled an earphone out from underneath his tousled hair.

'Sorry, mate, I dropped my pen. Could you...?' I pointed down by his boot.

He bent down and returned it, spinning it in his hand as he did.

'Any good, this?' he said, nodding at the front of the hall.

'Uhm, yeah, it's been pretty useful.'

'Awesome,' he replied, flatly, adopting cool-guy slouch #2.

I turned to face the lecturer again but the guy leaned across, whispering so close to my face I could smell his breath, feel the wet warmth on my cheek.

'What d'you think about that lot then?' He nodded

his head again, hands obviously too firmly wedged in his tight jeans.

I leaned forward and looked past him. Amongst the rows of students I couldn't work out who he meant, so I gave him a puzzled look.

'Blonde, black and brunette over there,' he said, winking.

I looked again, spotting three girls sitting diagonally in front of us a few rows away.

'Well, it's the back of their heads...' I shrugged.

'I know,' he said. 'That's the fun of it. What do you think? Mingin' or not?'

'Uhm, I don't really know, mate. Sorry.'

The mature student to my left hissed again and when I turned he shot me a look.

'You bent or something?'

I spun back round to the slouching cool-guy. 'What?'

He stared at me, eyes dark and small.

'Fuck's sake,' he muttered, shaking his head. 'I just asked you what you thought about them. Sorry, I didn't know you were...'

'I'm not, but what does it really matter?'

The guy laughed, the zip of his jacket jingling as his chest moved. The mature student cleared his throat loudly again but I didn't look round.

'Look, I'm just here to study, you know?' This time it was my turn to nod my head towards the lecturer.

His upper lip curled slightly and he went 'Pfft', turned away and put his headphones back in. I sat back and whispered sorry to the mature student, but he just shook his head and scribbled a quote from the lecturer down in his notebook. I tuned back in to what the lecturer was saying but couldn't really concentrate.

'... and any additional information will also be in the online help forum, which you will use your university details to log in to. Now, I think that pretty much sums up the introduction to the course. I've set aside a few minutes for questions if anyone has any?' He checked his watch and then scanned the crowd of eager/bored students.

'Anyone?'

'...'

'Is everyone feeling a bit shy today?' he asked, smiling. 'I rather thought that might be the case. Ah well, any road, you can email me any questions or queries – my contact details are in the handbook and my office hour is between one and two pm on a Friday afternoon.'

The mood shifted; people started to talk and check mobile phones. The lecturer, sensing this, clapped his hands together.

'Let's call it a day there, folks. Enjoy your first classes and please, go easy in the Union.'

A titter of laughter echoed around the room and everyone stood, pulling jackets and bags on. The lecturer left and soon the crowd followed, trickling out through the small doors. I walked behind the student who'd been sitting on my right and was strangely pleased to find I was taller than him.

As we walked through the door he let it swing back behind him rather than holding it open, and I caught it with my foot. Shaking my head, I pushed the door back and walked out into the hallway. The students had quickly cleared out, desperate to get back to their flats/halls/pints at the bar. Walking towards the outer doors I was still behind the same guy and as we got outside he stopped to light a cigarette. I walked past him, one hand in my bag, searching for my keys to the flat, and he looked up. We made eye contact for a moment and he said, 'Enjoy your books, fag,' before clicking his lighter and igniting the tip of his smoke.

I kept walking and after a brief stop in Sainsbury's to pick up some shower gel I was home, narrowly avoiding a sudden downpour. I clicked the kettle on to boil and sat down in the kitchen.

'You'll be studying your subject of choice with a group of like-minded individuals. University is where you will develop and shape who you are as a person.'

The lecturer's voice hung in my head: his eloquent, refined Glasgow accent like a smack in the face compared to the stereotypes I'd expected. Mum had teased that I would end up with a West Coast accent, but maybe one like that wouldn't be so bad.

'Like-minded individuals,' I repeated aloud and then laughed.

'You bent or something?' I said to myself.

The kettle boiled and I poured some water into the cup, splashing a little on the worktop. As I wiped up the spill I heard the front door open.

'Anyone home?' Ashley called.

'Yeah, in the kitchen here,' I shouted back.

She walked in, soaking wet, and sat at the stool on the other side of the kitchen.

'How was your first day then?' she asked.

I told her about my welcome meeting, about the guy sitting next to me, about the delicious irony of Glasgow, City of Culture, housing English students so utterly uninterested in books, and the notion of someone not actually wanting to stare at girls for a brief moment of time. She laughed and said, 'What a wanker.'

'What about your intro?' I asked.

'Meh, so-so, really. The same stuff by the sounds of it. 'University is where you will develop and shape who you are as a person' – that sort of thing.'

'I hope university develops and shapes who that guy is as a person,' I said, sipping my tea.

'Think of it this way,' she said, scraping her hair back into a ponytail, 'when we graduate and I'm defending human rights in the EU court rooms and you're teaching English to eager, promising young students, you'll never have to think about people who don't share your interests again. He's probably one of those, what is it, 7% of students who drop out in first year? Not even interested in the subject, off to waste other people's time elsewhere. The likes of us, Ben, we're destined for great things. We have dreams and ambitions and we're pursuing them. There's nothing wrong with going after your goal, no matter what it is. It's the ones who give up on theirs I can't stand.'

'Yeah,' I said, setting my mug back on the worktop. 'You're right there.'

'As always,' she said, winking.

4

The Auld Hole in the Wall is a traditional-looking pub on Linlithgow's High Street. All green walls and gold trim on the outside. An old-fashioned sign across the top says the name in block letters. The interior is fairly standard. It's got that old pub smell and I breathe deeply as I walk in. Stale smoke and lager. It's not that busy tonight, not yet anyway. Two old men sit at the bar, one at either end, staring into their drinks with sad, red eyes. The bar staff: a man in his mid 50s and a woman who looks to be about 20 years younger, stand chatting by the till. I look about a bit more but I don't see any of the guys from work so I lean on the bar and get my wallet out.

'Awright darlin', wit can I get ye?' The woman smiles as she walks over.

'I'll just get a pint of Tennent's, please,' I smile back.

She pauses and purses her lips for a second. 'Awright if I see some I.D first? Sorry tae be a pain but I huvtae.'

'Yeah, that's fine,' I hand over my passport, battered around the edges from nights out.

She looks over it and I see another smile brew at the corners of her mouth as she glances at my photo. 'Ha!

That's a belter. You look shocked tae be there!' she laughs and begins to fill a glass.

'Yeah, I never have looked good in photos. Family curse.'

'Yer a young lookin' twenty-wan, I'll tell ye that. Ye'll no' be complainin aboot gettin I.D'd when yer thirty.'

I smile, take the glass from her and hand over a fiver, hoping for more than three quid change. She comes back with a handful of coins, pours them into my palm and walks back to her colleague. I sip my pint and gaze around again. Still no faces I recognise.

'Ye waitin' fur a bird?' the old man next to me slurs. I look at him and he grins.

'Eh, no, just a few mates,' I take another mouthful from my glass and begin to walk over towards a table, away from the old man. I can feel him watching me so I sit down side-on, wary, keeping him in the corner of my eye.

A few more people come in and buy drinks or play pool, but still no one I recognise. It's half eight now and I'm checking my phone every few minutes. Eventually I crack and stand up, leaving my glass on the table. I bend over to get my coat and hear a voice behind me.

'Hope you're no' leavin' Benny-boy. The perty's about tae begin!'

I turn around and Niall's standing there grinning, hair gelled to extremes, with a suave-looking shirt on.

'The boys are at the bar gettin' the drinks in. Sit doon, sit doon. Jesus, they'll be over in a minute.'

I laugh as he pats me on the shoulder.

'I thought you guys weren't coming for a minute there.'

'Aw, we wouldnae stand you up, Ben. We were just roond at Jake's huvin' a few cheeky cans 'fore we came doon.'

Pete and Jake walk over to the table, carrying pints and shots. Pete, like Niall, is in a shirt and casual jeans. Jake's wearing a Roxy Music t-shirt and skinny jeans, his hair looking very '80s.

'Alright Ben?' says Pete, handing me a pint and a green shot, 'How're you?'

'I'm alright, ta. I was beginning to think you guys had cancelled on me for a minute!' I say, laughing again.

'Aye, well,' he scratches his beard, 'We just got carried away, having a wee chat, y'know? Debating. Intelligent conversation.'

'Great minds, we are, Ben. Great thinkers,' Jake chips in.

'Sounds good. What were you guys talking about?'

Jake and Pete look at Niall, who ignores them and launches straight in.

'I wis jist sayin' that there's nothin' wrong wi' bein' fae Scotland. It's a great wee place. All this rich culture an' history, y'know? Clans an' huge battles. Stuff like that. I hink it's great when you're at a wedding an' it's aw kilts an' sporrans. Makes me feel like part ae wan big family. Makes me feel safe. I can feel ma roots, ken?'

Jake's quietly giggling into his pint and Pete's scratching his beard with increasing vigour, two shot glasses, empty already, in front of him. I sit and sip my pint every few seconds, conscious that I have two to get through before the next round.

'It's no' jist aboot wearin' tartan an' hatin' the English, mind. I mean, I'm glad when I see them takin' a beating, that's fair enough, but there's mair tae bein' Scottish than that.' Niall pauses for a moment and stares at Jake.

'You still pishin' yersel' over this? Jist 'cause I'm proud tae be fae Scotland? Proud when I see that flag? Proud when I see that perlament?'

Jake stops laughing and stares back incredulously.

'The parliament? You're actually proud of that heap? Something that looks like a child made it? Look, Scotland is nothing to be proud of, Niall. I mean, just look about you – junkies scamming 20p's on the street, wee neds battering each other, folk with no teeth downing Irn Bru like there's no tomorrow. It's crazy, man. I mean, nowadays Scotland's just full of folk trying as hard as they can to kill themselves. Plain and simple. There's no glory here. No glens and heather. You're thinking of a different Scotland, Niall. One from the past. Like, for example, mind that taxi journey last month, when we went through Camelon? It was just full of different ways to fucking ruin your own life – tanning salons, betting shops, offies, pubs, takeaways. That's all Scotland is now. A fuckin' wasteland, full of a few different ways to try and kill yourself, and who could fuckin' blame you? The only ones not sucking shite in the gutter are the ones like you, full of this pride for a country they still think is full of *Jacobites* and *Rabbie Burns* and *Walter Scott*, but it's not. There's fuck all here except pride and dickheads.'

Jake takes a deep drink from his pint, thumbing the red Tennent's logo slowly. Pete is leaning back in his chair stretching and Niall's eyeing me up warily.

'So, Ben. Tell us, wit dae you hink aboot this wee place? This *proud shitehole*?' He pronounces the words grandly, eyes flicking to Jake.

'I dunno. I mean, I guess Scotland's just the same as everywhere else, really. We'd probably feel the same way if we were in, like, Essex or Brighton or somewhere, y'know? I think it's just that feeling that Scotland's shite 'cause it's all we know. I mean, at least it's not Bosnia or somewhere, I suppose.'

Niall's shaking his head slowly and staring at the empty shot glasses in front of him. I try to ignore him and continue.

'I mean, we're just four guys from Linlithgow sitting in a pub on a rainy summer night, having a few drinks, moaning about Scotland. There's probably four American kids somewhere in Kansas moaning that fuck all happens there, or a bunch of Japanese guys complaining about fucking Tokyo. I think we just feel this way because we're here, if you get me?'

'Aye, I see wit you're gettin' at, Ben,' Niall continues, 'but ma point is that it's *no'* shite. It's actually pretty gid. Like, fur example, where else dae you git songs like Loch Lomond? Auld Lang Syne? None ae these other places huv songs that end a perty like that, ken wit I mean? That's culture fur ye at least.'

Jake chokes on a mouthful of lager as Pete ignores the conversation, looking around the pub.

'So that's what's good about Scotland? Songs? Every country has songs, Niall. There's nothing special about a few wee tunes from Scotland, compared to all the rest of them.'

'Aye, but they've git nothin' like this. Nothin' that makes ye feel *proud* an' *alive* an' jist full ae *energy*. There's a sense ae vibrancy aboot bein' Scottish ye jist dinnae git anywhere else. Ken, when yer singing, it's almost like ye can hear aw the auld deid Scots jist singin' wi' ye. Like you're part ae an army, ready tae take on the world.'

Pete leans back in, towards the table, whispering.

'Fuck, boys, we'd better move.'

'... Like you're aboot tae go tae battle an' you're invincible because you're fightin' for *truth*, an' yer *people*, an' yer *homeland* ...'

'Boys ...' Pete says again, louder this time, rubbing his chin and glancing over his shoulder.

'... *Pride* an' *honour* an' aw that ...'

'Here!'

A voice shouts across the pub and cuts Niall off. We all turn and look. Three guys, a bit older than us, are standing by the doorway. Three massive guys blocking off the main exit.

'Here!' one of them shouts again, taking a step forward, 'Wan ae you boys pulled a blade on me last week.'

He reaches inside his jacket pocket and pulls out a small kitchen knife. Smiling, he turns it slowly in his hand.

'Well now it's ma turn.'

5

'Shit,' Jake says, looking round at us.

'Oi! None ae this pish in ma fuckin' pub. The lot of yous, out. Polis are on their way.' The barman stands behind his taps, his chest puffed, eyes fixed. 'Fuckin' move. Now.'

The group of lads look at the barman, the biggest one still turning the knife in his hand.

'Naw, we're no' leavin'. These dicks pulled a knife on me an' I'm no' lettin' them away wi' it.'

Niall tries to calm the situation, 'Oh fuck off, mate, that wisnae us.'

'Aye, it wis. Lithgae Arms, the other week. I remember,' the guy replies, swaggering forward. 'So where's the blade now, eh? No' got yer big mental tool tae protect ye's?'

A couple try to move towards the doors but one of the other lads glares them back to their seats. Jake speaks up, his voice cracking at the start.

'Calm down, mate, that just all got out of hand. We didn't want any–'

'I ken ye didnae want any trouble but yous fuckin' started trouble. So belt it.'

Pete gets out of his chair and the lad holds the knife up towards him.

'Not one mair fuckin' step.'

I look around for a door, a window, Christ, the hole in the wall this fucking pub is named after. There's a corridor leading to the back but I don't know what's there. Maybe a door outside, maybe a cleaning cupboard. I can see the barman still watching the group of lads, muscles tense. I turn back and see the other two guys have moved away from the door and towards Pete. Customers start running out behind them. Pete rests one hand on our table.

'Alright, calm it. I'm not going anywhere. Why don't we just think about this? The police will be here soon. If you leave now–'

'We're no' leavin' any time soon, pal.'

Pete's hand moves slightly. A twitch. Then another, more exaggerated this time. I stare at his hand and look at Jake, then Niall. They follow my gaze and we twig.

'Well, if you're here to stay, how about a wee drink?'

In a split second, Pete picks his empty pint glass off the table and hurls it towards the group. We don't hang about to see the result. We run, scattering our chairs across the pub, and head straight for that corridor, Pete leading. Behind us, I hear screams and footsteps on broken glass. Then, 'Fuckin' get after them!'

Pete pushes a door open and we're hit by the cold air outside. We look around, trying to spot a way out to the High Street, to an alleyway, to fucking Neverland. Shouts from inside the pub keep us moving.

'Over the wall, quick!' Jake says, already bolting towards it.

We climb up and I hear the door open behind us.

'They're off over that fuckin' wall!'

Looking round, I see two guys, the ones without the knife, run towards us, hands scratching for grip on the old stones. I slide over the top of the wall and drop down into the bushes below. Pete and Jake are already there, catching their breath, and Niall drops down seconds after me.

'Where now?' I ask.

Pete squints into the darkness, panting heavily. 'This way.'

We run through the bushes, skin scratched by thorns and branches, and it gets darker and darker. We come to another wall, smaller this time. I'm squinting so hard my eyes hurt and my skin stings from tiny cuts. We climb up and drop down to the other side.

'Where are we?' I ask, looking around. There's a set of mossy steps leading up to something I can't see, and a path leading one way to streetlights and another to thicker darkness.

'Fuck that – where are they?' Niall says, spitting on the ground.

We stand still and listen.

Nothing.

Nothing but our lungs overcompensating for the exercise and the occasional branch snapping in the distance.

Jake whispers, 'They must be lost in there.'

'Is there another way out?' I ask.

Pete shakes his head. 'That's the old arcade down the other way. They'd need to break in. Here...' He points to our left, down the path leading to street lights. 'What do you think, onto the High Street, or through the Peel?'

'Peel, definitely. It's pitch black and fucking massive. They'll never find us.'

We nod at Jake and continue along the path, half walking, half jogging. Our lungs burning, stomachs full of acid. The Peel is a big park, with Linlithgow Palace sitting at the top. Roofless and desolate, you can imagine Frankenstein inside; mad with power, screaming 'It's alive!' at his twitching monster. It's the last place I want to be in the dark and yet we head towards it.

'Fuckin' hell, man,' Niall keeps saying, still trying to spit the taste of exercise out of his mouth.

We reach the top of the Peel, by the Palace, and stop for a moment. There's just the gentle lap of wind blowing waves across the loch. No footsteps, no shouting. It's just us and the wind.

"Hink we're awright now?' asks Niall.

'Dunno,' Jake replies, squinting down a road leading back to the High Street. 'Wait,' he says, narrowing his eyes further, 'No. Look.'

Three figures walking up the road, near indistinguishable in the shadows, stop. After a second, they burst into a run. We turn quickly and head down the other side of the hill. Stumbling and slipping down the grassy slope, we eventually reach another path. It winds through an old gateway and alongside the loch. Birds awoken by our noise squawk and fly in clouds of confusion across the path. There's shit everywhere and I skid with every step. I look across my shoulder and see the boys gaining speed. Another skid. I feel my knees twist and buckle. One foot leaves the ground. No purchase, it cuts through the air in an arc. My arms wave out and reach for something, anything. I find a branch. My fingers close around it, the bark rough and cold on my skin.

Crack.

It snaps and my whole weight comes down on the concrete. With a dull thump I land on my hip.

'Fucking–'

I scramble up and try to run again. My left leg feels slow, as if the drinks earlier have focused solely on those muscles, weakening them until they can barely work. I struggle on, hip aching, clothes and hands slimy with excrement.

We cut through the Vennel flats and reach the road. Weaving through a line of traffic we make it across to the pavement. The three guys are still coming, having reached the spot where I fell, but not succumbing to the shit slide of a path. Niall turns to us.

'Look. Get on!'

We follow his gaze up the road. A bus is making its way closer to us. The front is poorly lit but we can just make out the info.

38
Falkirk Bus Station

Four hands are stuck out into the road and the bus pulls over. We get on and the driver gives us a withering look.

'Eh, four singles. Falkirk. Change is yours,' I say, as Jake, Pete and Niall head for seats near the back. I hand the driver a tenner and the doors hiss shut.

Sitting down next to Niall, I look through the window. The three guys are at the roadside now, gesturing with thick arms and shouting, though I can't hear what they're saying over the bus engine. The one with the knife points at us, blood streaked down his face, his finger stabbing the air angrily, and then dips a hand into his pocket. He hurls a coin after us and I hear a metallic crack as it connects with the rear of the bus.

I exhale loudly and look down. There's bird shit everywhere.

'Fuckin' hell, Ben. State ae you,' says Niall, half laughing, half panting.

'Haha, looks like you had a *shit* night,' Jake cracks.

Pete holds his phone up; the name on the screen reads Bruces' Taxis.

'Who's chipping in to get home then?'

6

Buzzing.

Buzzing and beeping.

I swat the duvet away and sit up. The room is blurry and filled with shadows. A rancid smell. I rub my face and touch my hair. It feels dry and matted with something, and then it comes back to me.

The pub.

The gang.

The knife.

The running.

The fall.

The bird shit.

I pull my fingers out of my hair and look at them. They don't look any different but I'm sure they'd glow under UV light or something. Bird shit everywhere. Still the buzzing and beeping and I look around the room. In my head I see a giant mechanical wasp bumping against the window but in my room I see my phone, lit up, buzzing and beeping.

Work, says the screen. I go to pick up but the call ends and the screen changes. 10 missed calls. I look at the time. 8:30a.m. My shift starts at 7:30a.m. Or, my shift *started* at 7:30a.m. Fuck. I run through to the bathroom and turn the shower on. I figure I'm late enough already; what's the harm in another five minutes if it means I won't be covered in shit when I do turn up? In the cubicle, the water is too hot and I flinch as it scalds me. Then it turns ice cold and I grimace. The temperature settles and I cover myself in soap and shampoo, my fingers working through the mess in my hair.

Back in my room, I quickly towel dry and put on my uniform. They gave me two complete sets and this is the first time I've worn this one. The material feels stiff but comfortable. The badge seems to glow bright green on my chest. It hurts to look at. It hurts to even see myself wearing this uniform; never mind with a hangover, a near death experience and a luminous badge thrown in. I lace my shoes and run downstairs. My parents must both have left for work already so I grab an apple from the fruit bowl, lock the front door behind me and start to run.

The streets are wet from rain in the night but the sun is out and glaring at me, making me squint my eyes as I jog. My head is pounding, almost in time with my feet, and my stomach feels tight and acidic. It's a half hour walk from my parents' house – my house – to Asda, so I reckon I can get there in twenty if I keep running.

I head along the canal, dodging dog shit and puddles as I run. There are boats tied up along the bank and they all have their curtains drawn. I'm jealous for a moment and then quite glad I didn't sleep on a boat last night. My stomach churns and tightens again. I check my phone as I run and see a text waiting.

09:01a.m. Niall.

Pauls gonnae fuckin kill you.

I turn down onto Back Station Road and pelt down the hill. When I was in primary school I heard a story about a boy who fell off his bike on this road. He was going at such a speed down the steep slant that when he landed he kept moving for the rest of the decline. They had to take him to hospital because he'd torn his knees to the bone.

I think about those online guides as I run; the ones about going to the gym after a heavy night of drinking. *Sweat off your hangover!* they say, like it's so easy. Right now I feel like I'm sweating off every drop of moisture in my body and the hangover is getting worse because of it.

I run past Tesco and see all the cashiers sitting bored, staring into space. School kids earning pennies to sit and do nothing all day but scan items and press buttons. Adults earning little more to do the same. I wonder what would happen if my parents earned the minimum wage. We'd probably lose the house. It's amazing anyone manages to earn their keep on minimum. Trying to knock the middle-class from my head, I keep running. Faster now. Past my old primary school, an old Victorian building with a new, modern back to it. Still looks like a borstal to me.

And then fields. Endless fields rolling from hill to hill, up to the horizon. The motorway cutting through farm land. The farm land enclosing the motorway. I run past flickers of green and yellow and green and green and eventually see Asda. White and green and glass. Standing, imposing, in the middle of what used to be another field: what is now a huge concrete car park. The locals, my Mum included, had started a petition to stop them ruining such prime wildlife habitat. They had hundreds of signatures and someone even egged the provost at the Marches to raise awareness, but it didn't help. The diggers moved in and soon enough the concrete was laid and the trolley wheels oiled.

The automatic doors whirr open and I jog inside, red-faced and panting. There's a horrible taste in my mouth and a good chance I'll be sick. I see Niall sitting at a till.

'Where the fuck huv you been? Paul's gonnae fuckin'—'

'Paul will deal wi' this hissel, Niall,' Paul's voice booms as he marches out from an aisle. He stops and looks me up and down. 'Where the fuck huv you been?'

I inhale deeply and cough as the air hits my lungs. 'Sorry, Paul. I'm so sorry. My alarm broke so I slept in.'

Paul looks at me again, surveying me like a falcon eyes a vole. 'Well ye can head over tae the electrical section an' pick yersel' up a new one. Dinnae let this happen again, Ben. You only git wan warning. Now go see the list ae things tae dae at the desk an' git fuckin' crackin'.'

He glares at me then Niall, and walks back to the office. Niall lets out a sigh.

'That wis close. Fuck's sake. Tell ye, I am fuckin' dyin' the day. Aw that runnin' aboot's left me wi' this beltin' headache.'

I laugh and walk over to the desk. Whoever is manning

it today has drawn all over the list of tasks. Niall's clearly bagged number one – cover the tills – and that leaves me with either sweeping and dusting or extra stock replenishment.

'You sure it's not all the drink that's left you feeling rough, Niall?' I ask, contemplating what will be easiest of the two choices.

'Naw, definitely aw the runnin'. I'm no' cut oot fur aw that. I mean, I love a wee game ae fives, of course, but no' runnin' aboot in the dark, feart ae gettin' stabbed. That's no' ma kindae game, ken wit I mean?'

'I know the feeling, yeah. Pete and Jake not in today?' I score dusting and sweeping off the list and look for the polish.

'Jake is, later on. Pete's day off,' Niall's resting his head on his arms, his voice muffled and low. 'I feel fuckin' horrible. Bunch ae dicks, chasin' us aboot last night. Fuck's sake.'

'Still can't believe what happened,' I say, shaking my head.

'Jist a bunch ae fannies tryin' tae act aw tough, ken? So wit, I pulled a knife on wan ae them? He wis startin' on Pete. It's *them* who kicked aw this aff – *them* who's wantin' a kickin', no' us.'

'D'you think this is the end of it?'

'Fuckin' hope so. I'm no' up fur a fuckin' midnight jog after every trip tae the Auld Hole. Means we're gontae huv tae find another pub now. That's two they've ruined fur us. The Arms an' the Auld Hole, fuck's sake. There's only nine left after that!' Niall looks genuinely worried.

As Niall talks, a woman approaches his till and sets her basket down. She unloads her items with a sneer on her face. I try to end the conversation, conscious of the customer.

'Ah well. Never mind, eh?' I duck below the desk and hunt for a duster.

'Naw, no' niver mind. I'm wantin' tae end this. I'm sick ae aw this. Aw this stress I huv tae deal wi', jist 'cause a bunch ae dicks like them are tryin' tae swing their weight aboot? No thank you.'

I stand up, duster in hand, and hear Niall say, 'Hiya luv', to the woman, who remains silent. 'Fuckin' hell, ma heid is killin' me,' I hear him whisper.

'Maybe it's all that foul language,' the woman snips. 'Do you mind? I'm in a hurry,' she motions to her items.

The air is tense and everything seems to slow down. Niall looks at the woman.

'Excuse me?' he says, eyebrows raised.

'I don't expect to hear that sort of language in a shop. It's rude.'

'I hink you're bein' rude. Did ye no' jist hear I'm no' feelin' well?'

'All your own doing, I suppose.' The woman glances across at me and I quickly start polishing the desk.

'Actually, naw, it's no'. I almost git fuckin' killed last night, so I'm a wee bit shaken. *Understandably so.*'

The woman purses her lips. 'I'd like to speak to your manager, please.'

'Aye, right,' Niall stares back at her.

'Now, if you don't mind.'

She isn't budging. I'm amazed at Niall's argumentative skill. He seems well versed in pissing people off.

'Fine. That's him there,' Niall points at me.

I freeze.

'Excuse me,' the woman calls across.

I stand still, duster hanging limp. I look up and force a smile. 'Yes?'

'This young gentleman,' she spits the word, 'is using foul and offensive language.' I can see her lip shaking slightly and I get the idea she feels out of her depth. I'm feeling about the same, in all honesty.

Niall stares at me, willing me to do something stupid. In my mind I'm saying 'Is he now? What a cunt' but in real life I'm stammering, 'Niall, eh, don't offend the customers. I'll have you in the office straight away.'

She looks back at him smugly. Niall smirks. My heart is thumping. I'm willing him to behave.

Don't say anything else. Don't say anything else.

'How fuckin' sad are you?'

'What?' she says, her mouth falling open.

'How fuckin' sad is your life that you huv tae moan about sumhin so *insignificant* as me swearin'? You dinnae even ken me, or wit I hud tae go through last night. It's half past nine in the morning an' I'm no' feelin' very well, awright?! Anyways, wit the fuck are you even daein' here? D'ye no' huv a job? A life? Fuck's sake, if I were you, I wouldnae be bitchin' aboot other people, I'd

49

be takin' a long hard look at ma ain fuckin' wreck ae a life before Googlin' ways tae fuckin' top masel'.'

Niall pushes himself off the checkout and storms past the woman, who looks on the edge of tears. I hear him as he walks away, spraying 'Fucks' and 'Jesus cocking Christs' into the air. I look to the woman, setting my duster down on the desk and apologise.

'I'm, eh, really sorry about him. He's not been himself recently. Eh, a troubled young man. Here, let me get those for you.'

I take over Niall's till and scan the items through. Then Paul steamrolls over.

'Ben, wit on earth's happened here?'

I explain to him that Niall and the woman had a 'disagreement' and that he left to avoid it escalating, but by now the woman is crying. Her mouth twisted, cheeks flushed, she's hysterical. Paul takes the woman into the office and tells me to tidy things up at the till.

After a little while the woman walks past me, eyes down. I wonder if she told Paul about me pretending to be a manager. My heart quickens and I imagine myself on the receiving end of a bollocking. Niall walks past a few minutes later and resumes his seat at the till. He sits silently for a few minutes, staring at the screen, as I make my way back behind the desk.

'You alright, Niall?' I ask.

'Disciplined,' he says after a long silence. 'Thought I wis gonnae git fired fur that. Got off lightly. Last warning, mind.'

We stand around for a bit, not saying much: both of us feeling awkward, as if it was us who had argued. Niall clears his throat.

'I wis hinkin', right?' he says, 'Ken last night, when we git started on by they lads?'

'Yeah?' I say.

'They were only after us. Like, they only kent oor faces; me, Pete and Jake. No' yours.'

'Yeah...' I repeat, wary.

'Well, I hink it's pretty sound that instead ae runnin' aff, pretendin' no' tae ken us, you stuck wi' us; git yersel' caught up in this mess.'

I don't say anything. My stomach clenches. I could have run away: gotten out before I'd even gotten involved.

'I hink that's really admirable, Ben. You're a sound guy. Wan ae the team, I'd say. I ken Jake an' Pete will agree. That wis a brave hing tae dae. Ye've proved yersel', 'specially tae them.'

Niall looks at me and I feel myself really, finally allowed into the group. Hazed, in a way. Like a college freshman accepted into a fraternity. Like a middle-class university graduate involved in gangs and knife-crime. Somehow, that doesn't feel quite as cool and glamorous.

'That wis a really brave hing tae do,' Niall says, tapping at the till screen.

7

Niall's engrossed in the till, probably reliving the disciplinary with Paul in his head. I stare at him for a while, replaying what he just said.

instead ae runnin' aff, pretendin' no tae ken us, you
stuck wi' us; git yersel' caught up in this mess.
you stuck wi' us; git yersel 'caught up in this mess
c a u g h t   u p   i n   t h i s   m e s s

I walk out from behind the desk, my head whirring, and head for the staff room.

'Just taking a break,' I mutter. Niall grunts in acknowledgement.

Walking towards the back of the shop, things feel weird; different now. Just by mentioning it, by saying the words out loud, Niall made it real.

There's no backing out now, I think. *They know your face, know your friends, know your work.*

I picture them outside, waiting silently in a car, the lights off, eyes fixed on the green glow of Asda and the halogen glare from the shop lights. Teeth gritted, they're waiting for the distant beep of the PA, Paul's voice sounding through the building: '*Right lads, that's us for the night.*'

Waiting for the lights to go off, the doors to be pushed open. We'll congregate outside as Paul locks up, saying our goodbyes. We'll be chatting, oblivious, as the car doors open and they step out, eyes locked on their prey. Then, cheetah-like, they'll pounce, tearing across the tarmac with blades like claws, and rip us to shreds before we know what's going on. Our bodies will be found the next morning, bones bleaching in the sun, a wake of vultures picking at our eyes.

I look up at the secure door to the staff area. Through the window, Paul is twirling his finger in the air and mouthing, 'Turn aroond. Back tae fuckin' work'. A movement to my left makes me turn and I freeze as I come face to face with an old man.

'You alright, son?'

'Yeah, sorry, miles away there. Can I help you?'

'I'm looking for light bulbs.'

'Ah. Eh, other end of the shop, I'm afraid. I'll walk you.'

Together, we walk towards the section which, much to my annoyance, is clearly labelled LIGHT BULBS and I direct the old man down the aisle.

'Is there any particular type of bulb you're looking for?' I ask, knowing full well there will be.

'One like this,' he says, holding his hand out to me.

Clutched in his stubby fingers is an old bulb, the glass yellowed, the print faded.

'Right...' I say, taking it from him. 'Just let me have a look here.'

'It's for my living room,' the man says, trying to help.

I examine the bulb, gathering only that it's a bayonet fitting. The print is too far gone to make out any specifics like voltage and wattage, so I just find the most common bulb on the shelf.

'This should do you, sir.'

I hand him the box and he squints, holding it at arm's length, to read the info printed on the side.

'Are you sure?' he asks.

No, I think. 'Yes,' I say. 'That should do you perfectly.' I gesture to the other side of the aisle. 'Have you got a smoke alarm?'

'It's not one of those energy saving thingies, is it?' The man ignores me, still squinting at the bulb box. 'I don't want any of that rubbish. Gives me a headache.'

'This should fit the bill then, sir. Just a simple, regular bulb.'

Just then, I feel a vibration on my thigh and I reach into my pocket. The old man turns and smiles a sparsely-toothed grin.

'Thank you, young man. You've been very helpful. A credit to your youth,' he chuckles. 'So is this just a wee job to help get you through college then? Or is it still school? I'm no good with ages.'

Me in my graduation gown, holding my certificate.
Mum crying. Dad looking at his watch.
Me picking my drink up off the living room table and
telling Dad about working in Asda.

Me standing at the front desk, polishing the wood in
large, slippery circles.
Instead ae runnin aff, pretendin' no tae ken us, you
stuck wi' us; git yersel' caught up in this mess

'Could be, couldn't it?' I say.

I walk out of the aisle and head back to the front desk. Niall is leaning back in his chair, staring up at the ceiling. Ignoring him, I make my way around the front desk to the security camera's blind spot, and crouch below eye level.

Outside there could possibly be a pack of wild animals, waiting to rip each of my stringy tendons cleanly from my bones. At home there could possibly be a fire, hungrily eating the A4 piece of paper that tells everyone I have studied books for four years at university in Glasgow. But here, in this small, condensed version of a regular-sized Asda, there are *definitely* reminders that so far, my life amounted to a slim wage slip at the end of the month and a green and white name badge, despite being promised otherwise by school, parents, university.

I pull the phone from my pocket and sit crosslegged on the floor. The screen is semi-illuminated. It reads 1 New Message. Niall.

Bored as fuck m8. Need 2 blow off steam. Oot 2nite?

I tap out a brief reply and hit send.

Me too. Hate this job. Maybe. Still feel rough from last night.

'Cheer up, mate,' I hear Niall call.

As I rise, he comes into view, the picture of lazy young staff. He's still leaning back in his chair, the backrest reclined.

'The face on you, pal. It's like you're the wan gettin fuckin' disciplined.'

I shrug.

'Fuck's sake, Ben. There's mair tae life than wit ye dae fur a livin'. Especially in a job like this. At the end ae the day, the world isnae gonnae end if you dinnae wipe they shelves. You're comin' oot the night, end of.'

'What about Pete and Jake?' I ask.

'Aye, they'll be oot an' aw. Wouldnae miss another fine chance tae git threatened an' belt roond this wee toon, would they? I'm jokin' – if yer worried aboot they lads, don't be. They've hud their fun. Now it's oor turn.'

My lips raise into a lazy smile.

'See, there we go!' he cheers. 'Christ, it's like gettin fuckin' oil ootae a stone!'

'Blood,' I correct him.

'Aye, well hopefully they'll be nae blood ootae anyhin.'

My eyes dart to the shop front, hoping that outside, this evening would be blissfully calm, with no cars waiting, no knives glinting, no *Jaws* theme tune.

'Oh fuck, back tae work,' Niall says, nodding behind me.

I turn and see Paul walking out from the manager's office, his hands in his pockets.

'Workin' hard, lads?' he calls down the shop.

'You ken us, boss,' Niall replies.

'Aye, well let's keep it up, eh?' His tone is tight, borderline angry. 'There's mair tae life than yer mates. I need this shop workin' like a well-oiled machine. I've already warned you once, Niall.'

'So ye're comin the night, aye?' Niall whispers as Paul walks past, sighing heavily.

Again, my eyes flick to the shop front; to the outside world, to the danger, the chances, the horror, the horror.

'I suppose I'm in now, aren't I? May as well have some balls and face whatever might happen.'

Niall's face darkens and he looks at the ground. 'Nothin's gonnae happen, Ben. Stop fuckin' worryin' an' come oot wi' yer pals.'

8

It's raining, so the boys and I run round the back of the West Port Hotel with our jackets over our heads. We'd been sitting in Katie Wearie's Bar for pre-drinks and Niall had got talking to some guy about writing novels, but at 11pm he downed his pint, pointed at the clock and rubbed his hands together.

''Mon lads, git they drinks down ye's an' let's git goin'. It's time.'

We dutifully drained our glasses and grabbed our coats, the barman saying goodbye as we left.

So now we're standing in the queue to Code, the club behind the West Port, trying to shield our hair from the drizzle. Jake's pawing at his fringe as Niall chatters about the bouncers.

'I mean, they're aw dicks, bouncers. Jist rough guys who've hud the sense tae make a livin' oot ae batterin' folk. Bit these guys an' me huv a wee *rapport* – an understanding. They ken I'm awright an' I ken they willnae gie me any bother.'

We move up in the queue, single file. Niall's at the front, talking back to us over his shoulder. Two guys in polo shirts, damp and shivering, are turned away and they squeeze past us, swearing. The bouncer looks at Niall. They're about the same age and actually look quite similar.

'Awright Niall, in ye go.'

'Cheers, Danny.'

The second bouncer – older, bigger, rougher – opens the door for Niall and nods as he walks in. Jake steps forward and is met by a hand pressed firmly into his leather jacket.

'Ye got I.D.?' Danny asks, looking Jake up and down.

'Yeah, sure,' Jake says, fumbling with his wallet.

'How many ae yous the night?'

'Uh, three,' Jake points behind him as Danny hands his I.D. to the other bouncer. He nods and opens the door again, allowing Jake into the welcoming shelter of the cloakroom.

'You git I.D. an' aw, pal?' Danny says to me, arms fixed across his chest. I hand the card over.

'Wit age are you?'

'Twenty one.'

He nods and I step forward. The door doesn't open, though.

'An' where huv yous been the night?'

'Just next door, at the West Port,' I say, sensing Pete step closer towards me.

'An how many yous hud?'

'Just a couple, mate. Only warming up,' Pete says, cutting his way into the conversation, giving me the same '*Fuck's sake Ben*' look my dad perfected years ago.

'Aye awright. Nae bother the night, lads, okay?'

We nod, laugh nervously and say 'No worries', then step inside. We leave our coats in the cloakroom and get our hands stamped with an ink picture. I can't work out what mine is: a devil – a clown.

Pete pushes the doors open and there's a rush of sound. Code's a small place for a club: about twice the size of your average living room, with a tiny dance floor, small bar and a dozen little tables littered around. Jake and Niall are sitting at a table near the dance floor, a line of shots ready and waiting in front of them.

'HERE WE – HERE WE – HERE WE FUCKIN' GO!' Niall chants as we take our seats. 'It is fuckin' heavin' the night, boys! Bound tae be a gid wan.'

Jake hands us two shots each, we clink glasses and drink down the aniseed burn.

'MORE!' Niall shouts and runs off to the bar.

'Seems someone's out to get hammered,' Pete says.

'Hammered already, Jesus,' says Jake. 'I swear he's getting worse. Never used to be this bad.'

I get up and look around for the toilets. There are two doors in the corner behind us: one with an outline of a woman in a skirt, the other an outline of a man with a big cock drawn on. I walk in and head over to the mirror. It's dulled and scratched but I can still see my reflection. I smooth my hair and check my teeth. The cubicle door opens and a guy walks out, buttoning his jeans. His chest is huge – about twice the size of mine – and his shirt buttons are straining to keep it all in. He gives me a sideways look and mutters 'Poof' before leaving. If I had a pound for every time.

Back in the mirror, my shirt's still a bit wet at the shoulders and I notice I've done the top button up wrong. I go to wash my hands but there's no soap and the sink is splashed with blood. All the years I've lived here and this is my first time in Code. What an impression. I walk off, shaking my head, feeling dirty. As I open the door I bump into someone on their way in.

'Sorry, mate,' he says, stepping backwards. 'Hang on. Ben?' He looks me up and down. He's in a white shirt, damp with sweat, and blue jeans with a pattern printed on the legs.

'Yeah?'

'It's me, Andy!' he smiles.

I can't place him.

'From school? I moved into your physics class in fifth year?'

'Oh fuck, yeah, hi Andy. How're you doing?'

I still can't place him.

'Not bad, not bad. Just enjoying my weekend, y'know?'

He's really animated and I notice his eyes are wide and bloodshot.

'Yeah, good for you, Andy.' I go to move past him but he carries on.

'So what're you doing these days? Last I heard you were at university.'

He stretches the word 'university' out, verbally italicising it.

'Yeah, I did English at Glasgow. I'm just at Asda now, temporarily, building up a bit of money. What about yourself?'

He beams a massive grin and I notice his teeth are stained yellow around the gums. Too many drunken cigarettes turned into a habit, I guess. A memory flashes up: 'the smokers' from secondary school, and suddenly I can place Andy perfectly.

'I'm a team leader at Tesco,' he says. 'Just got promoted last month.'

'Oh, congratulations. That's really good.'

If I remember right, Andy left school after fifth year and landed a job in Tesco, gradually moving up the ranks. And now, if I worked there with him, he would be giving me orders. Names form and splash through the air around me.

Larkin. Austen. Heaney. Gray. Orwell. Eliot. Hardy. Salinger. Bronte. Woolf. Shelley.

I know these names through and through. Their works. Their lives. And yet if Andy was at Asda and told me to wipe the shit off the toilet walls, I would. Andy, who had spent his five years doing just that. If you scrubbed hard enough, you would work your way up the ladder. Oh, to be a team leader. Thing is, though, he doesn't exactly seem like he's having a bad time. He seems happy. Something no amount of studying *The Society of the Spectacle* had made me.

'Sorry, I've gotta get in. Bursting for a pish. You know how it is.'

He pushes past, pulling his cock out as he does, and I

close the door behind me. I stand for a moment, deflated, and then shake the feeling off as the song changes to an upbeat dance tune. Back at the table, Jake and Niall are arguing while Pete watches the DJ, ignoring the conversation.

'No way. I can't believe you're saying *The Jungle Book* is better than *The Lion King*.'

'It is! It clearly is, Jake. Wit's no tae like? Ye've got Baloo daein' that wee dance ae his; Bagheera always lookin' out fur wee Mowgli; they burds that sound like The Beatles; that mental snake. It's a classic.'

'No. Absolutely not. Sorry. *The Jungle Book* is such a simple story. There's no depth to it. It's just a wee boy, lost in the jungle, playing with some animals. *The Lion King* has so much more: family feuds, murder, growing up, responsibility ... It's massive.'

'Right, so you're tellin' me Bagheera hud nae responsibility? Did he no' look efter wee Mowgli? Did he no' follow Mowgli through the jungle tryin' tae keep him oot ae trouble? An' murder? Eh, are you forgettin' a wee character called Shere Khan? Aw he wants tae do is eat Mowgli! *The Jungle Book* is an out an' out thriller. It's a tense story, thinkin' aboot it. Beats *The Lion King* hands doon.'

Niall slams another shot down as Pete stretches his arms out, his joints cracking. He sips his pint, fingers tapping the beat on the glass. 'This guy's belting out the hits, man. Cracking tunes.'

No one pays any attention and Niall and Jake carry on.

'But *The Lion King* is based on an actual, famous play, Niall. *The Jungle Book* is just some shite an old man came up with. There's no merit there.'

'Wit fuckin' play is this then?' Niall scoffs.

Jake hesitates and looks at me.

'Hamlet,' I say, and Jake nods, smirking.

Niall stares at Jake for a moment then slowly shakes his head.

'So that makes it better does it? Just 'cause it's a fuckin' rip off ae some auld play? *The Jungle Book* is aboot explorin' an' adventure. *The Lion King* is aw jist hyenas an' wee beasties runnin' aboot Africa. Even *Aladdin's* better than that.'

'Yeah, I'd agree with that one, Niall,' I say, leaning forwards in my chair, '*Aladdin* is a great film. Totally overlooked.'

'Pfft, *Aladdin's* nothing compared to *The Lion King*. It's just a silly wee love story,' Jake scoffs.

'It's about more than just love, Jake,' I protest. 'It's about class divide, for one. Just look at Aladdin: a poor young man, stealing just to get by. Then he gets this big chance to mix with the rich and powerful but he doesn't know how to fit in. Isn't that just perfect class distinction right there? Isn't that so relevant to today? He knows they'd look down on him because he's a 'street rat', so he has to hide his roots. Then you've got Jasmine: this poor girl who's being told she has to marry someone because it's expected of her. She's totally being forced into it. It's about rebelling against a patriarchal capitalist society.

You've got some big creepy dick with a parrot trying to marry her and she doesn't even get a say in it – then he turns her into a slave?! How can you say that's not a great plot? It's totally about power, sexism, class war. It's way bigger than 'just a story about love'.'

'You sound like Fidel there, Ben!'

I look at Jake blankly. 'Who?'

'Oh aye, you wouldn't have met him. Fidel was this guy who worked with us last year. Real name was Tom. One of they pretend-lefties – he kept going on and on about big corporations fucking society up, and how we should stick up for the working classes...'

'Even though we're aw middle class – fuck, both ae his parents were *lawyers,* Christ's sake – an' he didnae have a clue wit 'working' wis, niver mind 'working class',' Niall interjects.

'He was a total cunt,' Jake continues, to nods from Pete and Niall. 'Lazy fucker, full of all this Marxist theory, even though he worked for Asda. Turned everything into a fight about class and the economy and all that. I was just like 'Mate, fuck off. I come here to work, not to put the world right'. Eventually he left to do some wanky useless course at uni like Fine Art or something. Last I heard he got arrested for egging Topshop in Glasgow. Lost his cashier job in Currys.'

I laugh, although the uni jibe stings, and we all sit for a moment, listening to the music thump and throb. I look around and the club's even busier now. Everywhere I look – designer jeans, short skirts, fake tan, check shirts.

'Still doesn't beat *The Lion King* though, does it?' says Jake. '*Aladdin*, I mean.'

'Easily,' I say and we launch back into the argument. '*Aladdin's* got songs, magic, heavy topics; everything you want in a film. Plus, Aladdin's much more of an exciting hero than Simba.'

'Is he fuck,' says Jake, knocking back another shot. 'Aladdin's shite and you know it.'

'I hink both ae your films are shite, to be honest, boys.'

'Fuck off, Niall. *The Jungle Book's* a big pile of cock.'

A voice interrupts. 'Excuse me, do you mind if we sit here?'

We look up and see two girls standing by our table. One is pointing at a couple of empty chairs we've pushed aside. She's got shoulder-length blonde hair and vivid eyes, a bright red drink in her hand. She smiles at us. The other is standing slightly behind her, jet black hair straightened down to her ribs.

'Sorry, we didn't mean to interrupt,' the blonde girl says.

'Aye, well ... ye did. Tryin' tae huv a discussion here, fuck's sake,' Niall glugs at his pint, then stares round at us, incredulous.

'Oh. Right. Sorry. Never mind then.' The girls turn and leave, the blonde talking into the other's ear. We stare at Niall, who's oblivious, swallowing the dregs of his beer.

'Can yous fuckin' believe that? Fuckin' cheek ae

some people. Now, where were we?' he asks, drumming his hands on the table. 'I ken – mair drinks!'

He gets up from his seat, using the table to steady himself and starts to walk over to the bar.

'Jesus,' Pete says, rejoining the group from his DJ-watch, 'he's a fucking mess. Definitely getting worse. He never used to be this bad. They girls seemed nice too.'

'He's a dick, aye, but you're not much better yourself, Pete,' Jake points at the array of empty glasses on the table.

Pete grins and looks over to the hazy dance floor. 'Aye, well. I feel like a dance. You coming, Jake?'

I follow his gaze. The floor is crowded with people swaying together; pulsing along to the bass line like one giant heart. They all blur into each other as the next song starts. A heavy drum beat. A deep voice rapping. Girls pop and grind and guys flash American gang signs in the air. *Westside. Eastside. Thuglife*. They rap along, albino black.

Hands up like pistols now. The crowd is one writhing beast. Colours flashing, flesh merging. Smoke (steam?) rising up to the roof and then cascading down the walls. The DJ leans into the microphone. There's a squeal of feedback and then the low fuzz of indecipherable speech. The crowd screams, cheers, howls at whatever he said and then the music changes again and the bodies keep moving. Faster this time. Faster, faster. The bass is thumping so hard I can feel it in my lungs. I look back at Jake and Pete and they're both looking around with the same fuzzy grin that says 'This is fucking amazing. I am so wasted'.

We all grin at each other and then I lean towards them.

'Guys, I just have to say–'

'WHAT?'

'I JUST HAVE TO SAY, TONIGHT HAS BEEN MAGIC. I WAS WORRIED YOU TWO DIDN'T LIKE ME, BUT YOU'RE ACTUALLY SUCH COOL–'

A huge crash cuts me off. We turn to look, eyes searching around for the source. Guys with knives? A bomb, maybe?

Niall.

Niall, lying on the ground. Niall, surrounded by broken glass and spilt vodka. Niall, hysterically laughing as he scrambles to his feet, arms clawing for leverage, slipping and falling back on the floor. There's a couple standing near him, both soaking wet. The guy looks angry. The girl looks disgusted. Niall manages to stand up and tries to wipe his shirt down. The angry guy walks over, shouting, though I can't hear him over the music. Niall pushes him, shouting back, and finally the bouncers arrive. Arms looped around his shoulders and waist, two bouncers – neither of them Danny – pull Niall away and march him towards the door. I scramble out of my seat, knocking my pint off the table as I do so, and run after him. I shout as I push my way past people but the bouncers don't hear. I'm covered in spilt drinks and stumble over a stool on the ground. I get to the doors, through the cloakroom, and outside.

The cold hits me like a fist. I shiver instantly and pull my jacket on, wrapping my arms around my chest.

''Scuse me, you just threw my mate out. Where is he?'

The bouncer points towards the road. I walk down the path, my bones frozen solid. All I can see are blurry shadows and car headlights, but in the distance I make out a shape sitting hunched over on a wall. I stumble over and sit down, clearing my throat.

'You alright?'

Niall's staring at the ground, swaying slightly. 'Aye. Jist ... need tae ... Aye.'

'What's up with you? You're fucked, man. Wasted.'

'Jist ... blowin' off steam, ken?' He smiles to himself but his face can't hold the pose.

'Niall, really. According to Pete you're not usually like this...'

Niall puffs deeply, tight hands holding on to the wall. 'It's jist ... aw this,' he looks around. 'It's bin a really ... shite few weeks, man ... tryin' tae cope wi' ... aw this.'

'Is there anything we can do? Go back somewhere, put *The Jungle Book* on the telly?'

He doesn't laugh. Doesn't even raise his head. We sit silently for a while and then he coughs. He tilts his neck and looks at me. A moment of clarity. The cold is sharper, edges more defined. A camera lens focusing.

'See when you're in the shower, right ...' Niall starts, 'an' ye're washin' yersel, right ... Huv ye ever, y'know, like ... checked?'

'What d'you mean 'checked'?'

Niall looks like a lost child. 'Y'know, like ... done The Check. Like the doctor tells ye.'

'You mean...' I glance down.

Niall nods and takes another deep breath. 'Aye, y'know, checked the auld equipment.'

'Niall, no offence, but where are you going with this?'

His chest heaves and he looks around. Car headlights blaze past us, illuminating our faces in occasional flashes. I feel cinematic. We could almost be in black and white. Rain drizzles heavily on us, soaking us to the bone.

'... I found sumhin, Ben. In the shower. About a month ago,' Niall's voice cracks. 'I found a wee lump.'

9

'I found a wee lump.'

Niall looks at me. His eyes are wide, like he's pleading for something. Rain trickles down his cheeks and he looks very young; like a little boy, lost in the supermarket.

'Fuck,' I say.

Niall keeps looking at me, silent. His face is pale yellow under the streetlights.

'Fuck,' I say. 'What do you think it is?'

Niall doesn't say anything but I reckon I know what he thought, his soapy hands frozen under the shower head.

C – Ca – Can –

'Can ye keep this a secret?' Niall says, his voice almost lost in the rain now.

'Of course, Niall. I won't tell anyone, don't worry.'

He turns his head and stares at the ground. His back is heaving and I think he's crying. He retches loudly, a deep choking sound from his chest, and vomits onto the pavement. I put my hand on his back, feeling his wet shirt against my skin. He's really cold.

He vomits again, spitting afterwards, long strings of acidic saliva hanging from his lips.

'Come on,' I say. 'Let's get out of here, yeah?'

I take my jacket off and put it over his shoulders. He slumps down from the wall, his feet splashing in the puddle of vomit, and tightens the coat around him.

'Sorry,' he says.

We walk back to the West Port road. A police car pulls up and two men get out. One of them is watching us closely, as the other walks over to a large group of teenagers swigging beer from glass bottles.

'Just taking him home,' I say as we walk past. The police officer shakes his head like a disappointed parent. *You've not let me down; you've let yourself down.*

We cross the road and walk past the statue of Katie Wearie: a cattle driver, she used to stop for a rest and have a drink at the West Port, hence the statue. As we walk, Niall stumbles on a slab and sprays vomit over the effigy. He spits on the ground again and wipes his mouth on his hand.

'Remember ... Mind that time they found a body in the loch?' he says, watching the ground as we walk.

'That Celtic fan a few years back?' I say, wondering where Niall's going with this.

'Naw, naw. Remember, we would huv been wee – primary school age. Mind, they found a woman in the loch, floatin' face doon? Floatin' wi' aw the ducks an' swans an' fish an' that. Hur hair wis aw like that aroond her,' he puts his hands on top of his head and splays his fingers, like a row of little horns. 'Like a halo aroon her heid. She looked like an angel, floatin' there.'

'I don't remember,' I say.

'I do. I wis there when they found her. There when they pulled her oot ... drippin' everywhere, covered in reeds an' plants. I mind when they pulled her oot an' aw these adults were stood aroon tryin' no' tae let me see. I wis jumpin' an' dodgin', tryin' tae git a look at hur. I don't even ken why, bit I jist wanted tae see this angel they found in the loch. I wis only wee, y'know? Niver seen an angel before. So I ran aroon an' pushed through these folk in front ae me, an' I saw hur.'

He pauses and spits more vomit and saliva out as we walk towards the graveyard.

'I saw hur, an' I froze. Her eyes were still open, Ben. Like she wis still tryin' tae git a last look at life. An' I mind them draggin' her tae the stretcher, an' they turned hur aroon ... an' she looked at me.' Niall stares at me, his eyes glazed, face dripping in the rain.

'She looked right at me, right *through* me, an' I got this really cold feelin' in ma chest an' I thought tae masel', 'That angel jist saw ma soul'.'

He pauses for a while and all we can hear is distant shouting behind us, the sound of our footsteps and the rain getting thicker and heavier.

'I can still see hur, Ben. From time tae time, I hink I see hur – standin' aboot at bus stops, or in the warehoose at work, or in ma room when I'm fallin' asleep. Sometimes I kindae hink she's hauntin' me.'

Silence for a minute as we walk past the graveyard and then Linlithgow Academy, where I used to sit in class, dreaming of going to uni and starting a career and living in a posh flat in Edinburgh. I look up at the windows and picture myself in one of the classrooms, staring out into the rain. Then I blink and the boy is gone and the silence breaks.

'Sometimes I git this strange feelin'. I git this feelin' like I'm almost jealous ae that woman. I git this *sensation* when I'm down by the loch, like that's where I belong. Sometimes, when I hink I see hur, I kindae want tae ask hur if we could swap. If I could be an angel for a wee while, an' she could stack shelves an' git pished at the weekends an' niver make sumhin ae herself ... D'ye ever git the feelin' you're failin' at life, Ben? Like you should be so much mair than jist this?'

He waves his arms around us; wrapping us, the rain, the drunkenness in his disappointment.

'An' I hink that's mibbe how she felt.'

He swallows and coughs.

'I hink that mibbe when she dipped hur toes intae that water fur the first time, an' felt that cauld shoot up hur legs, I hink that mibbe that's when she felt maist alive – when she wis aboot tae die. It's almost funny, actually, that when I found the ... y'know ... when I found *it*, I wis in the shower, pretendin' the water at the bottom of the tray wis the loch, an' that I wis wadin' ma way in. An' I wonder, Ben, I wonder if she kent that I'm aboot tae die, an' that's why she wis in ma mind that day...'

He trails off and I look around. The streets are completely empty and rain is pouring down the tarmac, across blocked drains, and collecting in deep puddles.

'Wit am I gonnae do, Ben?' Niall looks at me, waiting.

'Well you need to see a doctor. They'll be able to tell you if this is something serious. There's a good chance it's nothing bad.'

'Nothin' bad?' He snorts. 'How can huvin' a fuckin' lump on yer baws no' be bad news?'

I don't say anything.

'Ben, I'm really fuckin' scared.'

'I know, Niall. Tell you what – you get an appointment and I'll come with you.'

'Naw, I couldnae ask ye tae...'

'Niall, I'll come with you. I don't mind. That's what mates are for, isn't it?'

We stand opposite each other for a moment, almost like at the end of a date.

'Thanks, Ben,' he says, looking at the ground. 'I really appreciate ... eh, I'd really like it if ye didn't tell anywan anyhin aboot aw ae this.'

'Sure, don't worry about it,' I say.

'I wanted tae tell the others – Jake an' Pete – but I jist couldnae. Couldnae tell yous as a group. But I thought you were awright, sound, a doon tae earth kindae guy, even despite wit they said. So I telt ye. I trust ye.'

He points at a house at the end of the road. 'That's me, so, eh, cheers.'

'Don't mention it,' I say, still stuck on 'despite wit they said'. Despite what who said? Pete and Jake?

'Eh, sorry about your coat an' aw,' he says, pointing at the sleeve. There's a large stain of alcohol and stomach acid.

'It's alright – get it back when you can.'

Niall goes to say something but then doesn't, turns, and walks over to the house, swaying and stumbling across the road. I pull my phone from my pocket.

7 missed calls. 3 text messages received.

The calls are from Pete and Jake, as are the texts.

Where are yous?

Where the fuck are you guys? Phone us.

Fucks sake Ben. Phone us now.

I press call and it dials Jake's number. He picks up straight away.

'Where the fuck are you?'

'Sorry, I had to take Niall home. He was wasted. Where are you guys?'

'We're outside Code.'

'Right. I'll be there in a minute.'

I hang up and break into a run. My shoes splash through the puddles and I think about that woman stepping into the loch, feeling the water ripple around her toes. A shudder cuts through me and I feel a stabbing pain in my side, so I slow to a walk as I cross the West Port road.

Code must have closed, or kicked a lot more people out, because there's a huge crowd outside, all standing soaking in the rain. Another police car and a van have pulled up and I can see fluorescent jackets mingling with the crowds, confiscating bottles and warning drunks. A group somewhere are singing the synth riff to a dance tune and gradually more and more people join in until it's so loud it's difficult to hear anything else. I shout for Jake and Pete but don't get any answer over the singing. My phone flashes and I open the message.

Behind you, dickhead.

I turn around. Jake and Pete are standing by the wall Niall sat on earlier. They're nowhere near the pool of vomit and I notice they aren't alone either. Two girls are standing with them, laughing and chatting. As I walk over, I realise it's the two girls Niall insulted earlier when they came and asked to sit with us.

'Benny-boy!' shouts Jake, wrapping an arm tightly around me. 'Look who it is!'

Both girls smile and say hi.

'This is Hannah' Pete points to the girl with long black hair. 'And this is Chloe.' The blonde girl smiles again and I stare at her teeth. They're Persil-white and perfectly straight.

'See something you like?' asks Chloe.

I realise I had just been standing staring blankly at her face and try to rectify the situation with my smoothest, sexiest voice. 'Yeah, your teeth.'

She laughs and looks at Hannah, who pulls a face and laughs too. My crisp, sober feeling from earlier has faded and the alcohol in my body is clearly getting a second wind.

'Right, Romeo, mind explaining what the fuck happened to Niall tonight?' asks Jake.

'Oh, he drank too much, threw up everywhere,' I point along the wall, 'and stole my jacket, so I took him home.'

'What a knob,' Pete says, turning towards the girls. 'Sorry about him earlier. Once you get him started it's hard to get a word in.'

'It's okay,' Hannah says, 'he did seem very into whatever he was talking about.'

'Disney films, wasn't it?' Jake laughs. 'What a prick.'

He casually puts his arm around the back of Hannah and rests it on the wall. She doesn't say anything. Chloe smiles at her and then me.

'So, Ben, is it? Pete and Jake tell me you're new here.'

'Kind of. Not really,' I say. 'I grew up here and then moved to Glasgow to go to uni, and now I'm back.'

'Ah, the lure of the Royal Burgh, eh?'

'More the price of the Big Smoke.'

'I bet it was more fun living in such a lively city though, wasn't it? All those parties?'

Did she just wink at me?

'All you've got here is a club that'll kick you out at the first chance and a bunch of pubs full of old men,' says Hannah, leaning into the conversation.

'That is true,' I laugh, noticing Jake shifting his hand from the wall to Hannah's back.

'So,' Pete says, 'what are you two up to now? Can't stand about in the rain all night, can we?'

Chloe looks at me, then Hannah, who shakes her head softly. Almost imperceptible. Almost.

'I'm afraid this is where our night ends, boys. We're just waiting on a taxi.'

Pete boos loudly and then laughs.

'Although,' Hannah says, 'we were thinking of having another big night out soon.'

'Maybe you guys would like to join us?' asks Chloe, flashing those teeth.

YES!

'Yeah, that would be cool,' I say.

A set of headlights shine on us and we all squint, hands up to our foreheads, into the glare. Chloe's phone buzzes. 'I think this is us, Hannah,' she says.

Jake trips on the kerb as we walk Chloe and Hannah over and a group of lads nearby shout and jeer. He rights himself, takes a bow, and keeps walking, grinning. 'Well I've had a great time tonight, ladies and gentlemen.'

'Except Niall acting like a twat, as usual,' Pete says.

Hannah opens the taxi door and gets in, nestling against the far window, as Chloe holds her phone out. 'Why don't you put your number in here, Ben, and I'll let you know about this party?'

I smile and shut one eye as I try to type the numbers in. Eleven digits – that seems right. Is that right? I try to recite them back to make sure she's got the right number. *She has to have the right number.* I'm really not sure if she has the right number.

'There you go,' I say, handing her back the phone. 'I look forward to hearing from you.'

'I won't make you wait long,' she says, climbing into the taxi.

I shut the door behind her and she waves through the window. The car revs and swings round before turning the corner at the West Port. I stare into the taillights until it makes the turn, and my mind drifts.

I see Chloe, wet from the rain, her phone in hand, dipping her toes into the loch. The water reaches to her ankles and she shivers. Her dress floats around her thighs as she continues to lower herself. Through the water, I can see her toes reaching out for the bottom, but instead they keep sinking further and further down into the darkness. Before long, it's just her head above the water and she glances up at me. She smiles and the water rises up to her beautiful teeth. I smile back and reach out my hand, palm open, waiting for her to take hold of it. Then her face changes and her skin looks cold and wrinkled: her eyes dead and watery. Her nose goes under and now it's just her eyes staring up at me. I'm trying to read the emotion in her gaze – maybe fear? Sorrow? Panic on the streets of London? – but her head slips under with a slight splash and then Jake's there and he says 'BEN! Ben, are you fucking coming with us or not?'

The world comes lashing back. The rain. The cold. The empty feeling.

'Sorry, I was miles away there,' I say.

'Yeah, we'd guessed. C'mon, Casanova, we're away home.'

10

Paul's staring out the front windows of the store. He checks his watch and then looks back up to the windows. It's raining, still, but it's gotten much heavier since last night. It seems like something else now – like at some point it stopped being just rain and turned to a full-on biblical downpour. As I walked to work this morning the streets were like streams, winding together, washing away the dirt. I arrived, soaking, and was met by Paul, who was using paper towels to dry his hair.

'If this keeps up...' he had said, glaring, trying to scare the rain into stopping.

Jake's working the warehouse today and I'm on till duty because the boy who usually does it is still off sick. Niall had scoffed when I asked him about it the other day, saying he was a 'skiving twat', but apparently he really does have jaundice. Paul's still in front of the windows, staring out into the wall of rain.

'He's late,' he says, breaking the silence between us.

I look over at him and he repeats it.

'He's late. Niall. Late.'

I think back to last night.

Niall doing shot after shot. The sink covered in blood. Arguments about films. Niall being rude to those girls. The lights and smoke and music. Niall crashing into that table. The bouncers carrying him out. Me, outside, looking for him in the rain. Sitting on the wall. 'I found a wee lump.' Niall vomiting over and over again. Taking him home. Niall stealing my vomit-sodden jacket. The girls back at the club. The girls back at the club. The girls back at the club ... Chloe ... and ... Hannah? Hannah. Chloe. Chloe.

CHLOE

I linger on her for a moment, remembering the cut of her cheekbones, the shine of her eyes, then focus. There is no way Niall will make it in today. Pete's still staring out of the window. He's shaking his head.

'Last fuckin' warning, I telt him. Last fuckin' warning.'

I glance down at my phone to see if Niall's texted me. He's not.

'Put that away, Ben. You're still on thin ice offae bein' late last time. An' if Niall does ever turn up you'll find oot wit happens when that ice shatters an' aw.'

He glares out at the rain again and it seems to get heavier as he does. It's so loud on the roof that the radio is completely drowned out and I can see a small lake forming in the car park. It creeps up and out towards the few cars still parked outside.

I notice someone at the far end of the car park. They're walking carefully, trying to dodge puddles and overflowing drains by the side of the path. As they walk by the lowest point of the car park, where the lake is growing, they slow down. They must be soaked, I think, and I wonder why anyone would come shopping in this weather anyway, never mind on foot. They trip on something and stumble. Their arms wave out in front of them but there's nothing nearby to catch on to. They splash down into the lake and land on their front, face submerged.

I flinch as it happens and Paul does too.

'Fuckin' hell!' he shouts, pointing. 'Did ye see that? See that dick jist fall there? Fucking hell, poor bugger.'

We're both laughing despite knowing that if it had happened to either of us it absolutely would not have been funny. Paul and I keep watching as they stand back up and start walking again, towards the shop. They're wavering slightly and stumble again a couple of times, looking around to see if anyone noticed. Paul's still chuckling but a realisation creeps up on me.

The person outside is in a dark jacket. A dark jacket which, as they get closer, has the same green piping as mine. Paul's still chuckling but slows to a stop when the automatic doors whirr open and Niall walks in and says, 'Awright Paul? Sorry I'm late. I jist, eh ... slept in, ken?'

Paul's stare could have lit Niall on fire if it wasn't for that wet fall a minute ago.

'See me trip outside there?' Niall continues. 'Fuckin' soakin', man. That burn's aboot tae burst an' aw, by the way.'

Niall's swaying on the spot and reaches out to steady himself on a nearby Pepsi display.

'Niall, wit the fuck are you daein'?' Paul says, pausing for a moment to survey the soaking mess in front of him. 'Are you pished?'

Paul's voice fills the shop and I'm glad there are no customers in. Niall sways, looking around the shop. 'Nice an' dry in here. No' like outside where it's aw, eh, wet an' that...'

Paul takes a step towards Niall and sniffs deeply. His nose wrinkles and his face twists to a sneer.

'You're late. And pished. I telt you, Niall, after you were a dick tae that wuman. I telt you you hud wan last chance. WAN LAST CHANCE!'

Paul's face is flushed and I can see his chest rising and falling rapidly. Niall's still swaying, dripping with rain, a puddle forming around him.

'This is fuckin' ridiculous,' Paul says, exhaling loudly, shaking his head.

'With aw due respect, Paul, I'm no' *that* pished...'

'No' that pished?! NO' THAT PISHED?! Ye cannae even fuckin' walk straight!'

'I wis daein' awright, give or take a few wee ... *incidents*...' Niall belches loudly. 'Jist calm doon, Paul, it's no' that big a deal.'

'It is a fuckin' big deal, Niall. You've gone aff the fuckin' rails recently! I used tae be able tae count on you tae do at least a half-arsed fuckin' job ae hings. But recently you've been, tae put it frankly, *fuckin' shite*.'

The last two words echo around the store and I press send on my phone. The message I tapped out as Paul shouted reads To: Jake. Niall's drunk. arguing with paul. get here now.

'I hink we aw jist need tae calm hings doon a wee bit here,' slurs Niall, leaning on the display until it creaks.

'I hink you need tae go an' pack your fuckin' locker, Niall,' says Paul, grabbing Niall's arm.

Niall shrugs his shoulder but Paul doesn't let go.

'Git affae me,' Niall moans, still jerking his arm.

Paul tries to grab hold of Niall with his other hand but Niall frees himself and pushes out, hitting Paul square in the chest. Paul stumbles backwards and then stands fully upright, looking Niall up and down.

'You jist made a fuckin' big mistake.'

I run round from my till and stand between them, arms outstretched. 'Woah, guys, just hold on a minute.'

'Ben, jist you stay outae this. I'm fine,' Niall says, puffing his chest, one hand still on the display.

'Niall, go an' pack yer stuff. You're fuckin' finished here,' Paul says, eyes fixed.

'Paul,' says Niall, slowly, still eyeing him like a boxer before the bell rings, 'away an' fuck yersel'.'

I feel the full weight of Paul's body against my outstretched arm and I dig my heels into the ground to hold him back. Niall swaggers off, pulling products off the shelves and opening them or throwing them to the ground.

Jake comes through from the warehouse. 'Paul, have you looked outside?' he says.

Paul loosens up and looks over at him. 'Aye, great, it's rainin'. I've git a lot on jist now, Jake, so–'

'Eh, no, not just that. The burn at the side of the shop?'
I remember Niall slurring as he came in.

That burn's aboot tae burst an' aw, by the way.

Paul sighs and I know exactly what Jake's about to say.

'The burn's flooded.'

'For *fuck's* sake,' Paul vents. 'Right, you two go an' grab they sandbags sittin' oot there an' try tae build a wall or sumhin. Dinnae let the water git intae the shop, right?'

We nod and run out the back. There's no sign of Niall so I presume he actually did walk off to clear his locker out. Behind us, I hear Paul yell and kick the display Niall had been leaning on. The stand buckles and sends bottles of Pepsi across the floor.

In the warehouse, we grab luminous jackets and pull them on. We walk outside but our feet are splashing in a layer of dirty water a few inches deep. We're too late. Jake looks at me. 'What do we do?'

I look back, blank.

'Fuck, uhm, right, we'll build it here, by the door,' he points to the entrance of the warehouse, where the shutters roll down at night.

The sand bags are outside, excess stock from the children's summer play range, and despite the jackets we get soaked walking back and forth. The bags are wet and heavy, some of them burst open, and they leak red, blue or green sand all down our backs as we carry them. Gradually the pile gets bigger and resembles a small wall that we're strangely quite proud of.

'What was happening with Niall?' Jake asks, trying to block a leak in the wall.

'He turned up really late and really drunk.'

'Oh. Shit. Did Paul realise?'

'Oh yes,' I say. 'He realised and fucking lost it. Fired Niall.'

Jake stops packing the bags and looks up. 'No way. Fired him?'

I nod.

'Fuck's sake. What was he thinking coming to work drunk? I mean, I know he can be a bit of a dick sometimes, and believe me, we've known each other for ages – you don't even know the half of it, but fucking hell...' Jake shakes his head, his fringe swaying in long, wet locks.

'Just carried on from last night, I guess,' I say.

'How was he when you took him home?'

'Fucked. Chucking up everywhere, but he didn't seem any better for it. He was a total wreck.'

Jake keeps shaking his head and saying 'Fucking hell.' We pile sandbags higher and wider across the warehouse floor.

'Here, have you heard from those girls at all?' Jake asks, stretching his back.

'Not a peep. Can't even remember if I got my own number right. Probably not, given the state we were all in...'

'At least they weren't after Niall's number,' he laughs. 'What a fucking mess. That Hannah got mine though, so we're both in with a chance.'

We finish the wall, having run out of sandbags, and

step back to look over our design. We're still splashing in water and if anything it's just gotten deeper. The laces of my boots are submerged and the insides are soaked.

'Fucking hopeless,' Jake sighs.

I nod. Just then, the PA system beeps and Paul's voice cuts through the shop.

'We're gontae huv tae shut the shop, boys. It's flooded roond here an' aw – manager's office, training room, Linda's office – the whole lot. Meet me at the tills.'

We look at each other, both wondering where Niall is now, and splash out of the warehouse. When we get on to the shop floor it's clear the burn didn't burst in just one place. The warehouse, where Jake first spotted the water, is downstream from the office-side of the building and there's been a huge flood at that end too. The aisles are like shallow streams now and the water laps around our ankles as we wade through to the tills. Paul's standing there, one hand spread against his forehead, his eyes closed.

'Right, lads,' he says as we arrive, his voice tired and small, 'this is clearly a massive fuckin' disaster an' it's gonnae take mair than jist us tae stop it. I've phoned this company who're gonnae come an' try tae fix everythin',' he gestures to the shop around us and kicks one foot, splashing us both with water.

'D'you want us to stay and help out?' asks Jake, genuinely.

'That's wit I'm aboot tae say – I've phoned head office an' they telt me tae shut up shop until it's aw fixed.'

88

'How long will that be?' I ask.

Paul sighs. 'Could be a couple ae weeks, could be a couple ae months. Either way it's gonnae be a fuckin' while. This water will take a while tae pump oot an' then we're gonnae huv tae empty shelves, write off stock for the insurance people ... It's gonnae be a big job.'

Jake looks at me and we stand in silence for a while, listening to the rain batter the roof and the burn roar.

'So what do we do now?' Jake asks.

'Now?' Paul looks around, considering. 'Now yous can go hame an' tell that fuckin' mate ae yours he's no' welcome here again.'

'Has he left then?' I say.

'Aye, packed up an' fucked off, still pished as fuck, calling me a wanker an' aw that ... Now I ken he's been gid before aw this an' he's a mate ae yours, but that's jist no' on, an' I willnae stand fur it, right?'

We nod. Paul stretches his arms and looks towards the door to the offices, where little waves spill out to the shop floor. He shakes his head again.

'He's no' right anymair, that Niall. D'yous ken if sumhin's happened tae him or anyhin?' he asks. 'Trouble at hame? Somehin like that?'

I found a wee lump.

'Not that I know,' says Jake.

They look at me, expecting me to provide an answer, but I'm staring at the door to the offices. I'm sure I saw, just for a second, someone standing there. Little ripples spread out and my eyes focus on them. There was a woman, I'm certain. A woman, her hair wet and hanging limp, standing watching us. I keep staring, willing her to come back, until my eyes blur and I blink and the doorway is definitely empty and the ripples have stopped.

'Sorry, what?' I say.

'Has sumhin happened tae Niall? He's fuckin' changed. Niver used tae be like this.'

'Sorry, I have no idea. He's not mentioned anything.'

Paul shakes his head and walks over to the automatic doors. Jake checks his watch. Paul looks at us and sighs another heavy sigh. He pries the doors open and stands between them.

'Right, go an' get yer stuff. I'll phone ye's when I hear wit's goin' on wi' the shop. There's fuck aw we can dae tae stop this now, so we'll jist huv tae wait an' see. Fur now, mind, we're officially shut doon, boys. Full pay, as far as I ken.'

'Bet you love your job on days like these,' I say, and Paul sighs.

'I actually love this job. The work's easy, pay's awright, banter's nae bad. There's worse jobs tae be hud, ken? But aye, days like these I jist want tae smash the place up.'

Paul surveys the flooded shop like a general looking across a battlefield.

'Aye,' he says, 'always remind yersel' things could be worse, eh?'

11

'Aww, wit's it?' he twists his hand, trying to coax the next sentence out. 'Ah – '*You take ma life when you do take the means whereby I live*',' Niall says. 'Aye.'

'Did you just quote Shakespeare?' I say, taken aback.

'Me an' you are no' that different, see,' he says, grinning. 'I did a bit ae auld Shakey in High School.'

We're rattling along the back roads to Livingston on the bus and Niall still hasn't mentioned anything about his appointment. Instead, he's talking about the shop shutting down.

'It's crazy that wan wee storm can dae aw that.'

'I know. All that water just bursting in. It's gonna cost Asda thousands.'

Niall shrugs. 'Disnae make that much difference tae me wit they huv tae pay oot. I'd jist be pissed aff aboot bein' left in the lurch, ken?'

'Yeah, I know what you mean. It's ridiculous that they expect us to accept a position in Falkirk and pay the expenses of getting there and back every day. I mean, I know it's not that much but the rail fares are going to add up in the end.'

'It's either that or tell em tae take their job an' shove it, I suppose. I mean, Fawkirk? C'mon ... I'm actually kindae glad Paul let me go.'

Niall's gazing out of the window, watching the fields zip past as we bump our way towards the town. I turn my head and find an old woman staring at us. Her face is cracked with lines, her stillness like she's carved from wood. Eventually she blinks and looks away, pursing her lips.

'You ok?' I ask Niall.

'Aye, I'm awright.'

'How're you feeling about today?'

Niall sighs and glances back out of the window for a second. 'I suppose it's better tae ken, than no' tae,' he says. 'At least this way I can stop ma mind fae always hinkin the worst.'

'D'you know what's going to happen? Y'know, at the appointment?'

'Like, wit are they gonnae dae tae me?'

'Yeah. Like scans or something?'

'The doctor jist said it'd be like wit wimen get when they're pregnant. 'Cept the nurse'll no' be sayin 'That's a strong, healthy heartbeat' an' aw that. Well, I hope no'...'

We laugh but he quickly loses his smile.

'D'ye ever hink aboot wit it'd be like tae be an animal?' he says.

'I can't say I ever have, no.'

'I hink they must huv such simple lives, y'know? They git tae jist sit in fields eatin' grass aw day. That's aw they huv tae hink aboot. *Where's ma next clump ae grass comin fae?* An' if it rains like this they git taken away inside. Nae worries aboot losin' a job or anyhin like that. Nae worries aboot fuckin' ... lumps.'

He sighs again. 'Ye'd hink fur the maest evolved species on the planet, humans would be a fuck ae a lot better at dealin' wi' aw the shite we get.'

'Did the GP say anything else?' I ask.

'No' much. I wisnae askin' questions either. Some fuckin' stranger wi' ma baws in his hand. I didnae really want tae stick aboot, y'know? I mean, it didnae matter it wis a man daein' it – ye ken me, I'm no' homophobic or anyhin. I mean, I've even been tae The Polo Lounge once – it wis just so fuckin' surreal.'

He pauses and shakes his head.

'I mean, there's me, jeans aroon ma ankles – fuckin' Superman boxers on an' aw – wi' ma baws jist hangin' oot, holdin' ma dick oot the way so the doc can huv a right gid feel. An' on the other side ae the window is the play park I used tae go tae when I wis wee. An' I could hear aw the bairns laughin' an' screamin' an' huvin' loads ae fun and I thought *that used tae be me*, y'know?'

Niall glances over my shoulder and I turn around. The old woman is staring at us again.

'Sorry, did ye miss a bit ae that? Want me tae repeat it?' Niall says, glaring.

The woman purses her lips again and looks down into her lap.

'Naw, dinnae act like ye werenae, ya nosey cow. I saw ye.'

She keeps her eyes fixed, lips pursed, and faintly shakes her head.

'Right, well jist let me ken when you're wantin' tae listen back in an' I'll make sure tae turn the volume up.'

Niall turns back and stares out of the window again. 'State ae some folk ... Wit is it about buses that jist makes every cunt start starin' aroon like neb'dy can see them daein' it? Aye, that's right, love, I'm talkin' aboot you!' he shouts across.

'Gonnae keep it down back there?!' the driver shouts.

Niall bites his lip and I apologise as a bell rings. The little screen shows the word STOPPING in orange pixels and the bus slows to a halt. We stand up and walk out in front of the old woman, muttering thanks to the driver as we step off into the wet greyness of Livingston.

The hospital stands solid and boxy; the generic design of the 1980s. Walking towards it, Niall checks his phone – the third time in as many minutes – and tells me we're early.

'Suppose there's fuck aw else tae dae though. Might as well go in,' he says.

The automatic doors hiss open and we walk inside. There's a reception desk in front of us and signs hanging from the roof. We both look at the signs and then down to the painted lines on the floor.

'Where d'you have to go?' I whisper.

'Shit. I cannae mind.'

'D'you want to go and ask?' I nod towards the receptionist and Niall looks at me, shaking his head.

'An' wit am I gonnae say, 'Awright, I'm here tae git ma baws looked at'?'

The receptionist looks up as Niall says this, and smiles. 'Can I help you?' he asks.

'We're looking for, eh, scans,' I say.

'Radiology.'

He points the way and we walk down the corridor, our shoes squeaking, following the line.

The hospital is quiet. I suppose it's better than if the corridors were full of screams and moans, but even so, it makes me feel like I'm a child out of bed at night. Niall's peering through every window we pass. More corridors branch off through double doors on one side, and on the other I can see outside the hospital.

'Fuckin' hell, this is a trek,' Niall says, sighing. 'Like wan ae they Japanese death marches.'

'Don't say that.'

I look out of the window at the road outside and feel a twinge in my chest; a tiny flicker of desire to leave Niall to do this himself. It passes and I concentrate on how I would feel if this was me, if this was my appointment, if those were my balls.

Niall's breathing heavily and we turn a corner.

RADIOLOGY

He stops outside and checks his phone again. 'Nearly time,' he says.

'D'you want to go grab a seat?'

'In a minute. Jist ... eh ... jist geez a minute.'

'Course,' I say.

We stand there for a while, Niall staring down at the

floor, breathing in slow, heavy breaths. I lean against the wall, looking into the radiology department through the window in the door. Inside, there are three people waiting. Each of them, like Niall, staring at the floor. A nurse walks over to one of them – a small old woman – and motions for her to go through into a room to the right. She stands, taking a while to get to her feet, and follows the nurse, leaning heavily on her cane as she goes.

'Right,' Niall says, his eyes now fixed on the door, 'let's go.'

He pushes the door open and steps inside. His face looks stern as he looks around. For a moment I imagine him to be a warrior going into battle; steeled and ready for combat, mentally preparing himself for the fight.

'Can I help you?' says a man to our left. He's sitting behind a desk, looking at a computer screen.

'Eh, aye. Niall Robertson. I'm a wee bit early.'

'Take a seat,' the man says, still staring at the screen in front of him.

'Right, ta,' Niall says, before walking towards the row of seats against the back wall.

The old woman is still in the other room and Niall takes her seat. I sit down next to him and look at the selection of magazines on the table. The covers are all emblazoned with real life stories about dead babies and jilted fiancés, so I leave them where they are and look around the room.

There's an area in the far corner which has a small red plastic table, two chairs and an array of children's books on a stand against the wall. There are toys scattered around the floor and there's a little girl playing alone, sitting in amongst them. She's telling a story to herself as she pulls small white teeth out from a snapping crocodile's mouth. Further along our row of seats, there's a young woman sitting with a child's play-bag, watching the girl and smiling. She looks on the edge of tears and I wonder how many other children have come here to play while their parents get diagnosed, or how many children have played with that same crocodile, pulling teeth out one after the other until the jaws snap shut and they laugh, until the nurse calls their name and they toddle into the room to be scanned and tested themselves.

'Ben,' Niall says, clearing his throat.

I look up at him but he's still staring down at the floor. 'Eh, I jist wanted tae say, it's pretty sound ae you tae come wi' me tae this. I mean, eh, ye didnae huv tae, an', eh–'

'It's alright, Niall,' I say. 'I wasn't going to leave you to do it yourself.'

'Aye, well that's wit I mean. Pete an' Jake are awright an' aw, but there's a wee part ae me that hinks they wouldnae huv done the same as you, ken? I've kent them fur ages now, fae workin' at the shop, but sometimes I jist hink we're no' actually that similar, me an' them.'

'What d'you mean?'

'Sometimes I hink – an' dinnae say nuhin tae em aboot this – but sometimes I hink they dinnae actually like me that much.'

'Like how they don't like me that much?' I ask.

Niall squirms. 'Ye remember that, eh? Can't believe I went and said that. It's nothin', Ben, jist stupit lad chat when ye first started. Ye've proven yersel' now, mind.'

I raise my eyebrows.

'It's jist, wi' you huvin' been tae uni an' aw that, they figured you were a bit ... kindae ... snobby, ken? Jist wary that you'd hink you were better than workin' in Asda 'cause ae your degree. But efter wit happened in the Auld Hole I hink they'll see you're jist the same as them, as us.'

Niall looks back at the floor and I think about how I felt when I first took the job at Asda, realising that they're right – I did think I was better than that. Maybe even still do. I think everyone's better than that.

'So what makes you think they don't like you?' I say. 'Fair enough me, I'm some poncy twat with a degree, but you?'

'Jist wee hings, y'know? Like them chattin' away at work an' then when I come over they stop – stuff like that. I mean, we're still mates, but sometimes I jist hink I'm no' as 'in' wi' them as I should be.'

He pauses, sighs.

'I kindae worry aboot a rift, ken? Like, they'll splinter aff an' we'll no' be wan group ae mates anymair. An' dinnae take this the wrong way, but now that you're here, I hink it's mair likely tae happen. Like before, when you didnae work at Asda, I jist let the wee hings slide, but now I feel like I've actually got somewan on the same sort ae page as me, ken wit I mean? Like if they act like dicks I huv somewan tae talk tae aboot it. Like I almost dinnae need tae put up wi' them anymair. I mean, I ken we've no' kent each other that long or anyhin, but it's like we've got the same sortae outlook on life, in a way.'

'D'you really think they'll just cut you off?' I say, eyes flicking to the little girl, who's now singing a song to herself.

'Kindae. I jist hink, an' it's mibbe me bein' paranoid, but sometimes I feel like we've jist got different ideas aboot stuff. Like how Pete's a wee bit older than us but he's still daein' the same old shite he did when he wis seventeen. I'd hate ma life tae end up like that, an' Jake seems happy enough tae let his life turn intae Pete's. I jist feel like sometimes I'm the only wan who wants mair than jist that shitey small toon and that shitey small club on a Saturday night. Dinnae get me wrong here, I dae like a wee drink an' a dance on the weekends, but I'd like tae huv a bit ae variation in ma life. Mibbe go tae Glesgae or Embra every noo an' again. The furthest they two will go is Fawkirk, an' that's jist the same auld small toon shite in a slightly bigger toon than oors.'

'I had no idea you felt like that,' I say. 'I mean, I feel the exact same. Like, a wee shit job is fine for now, but I want something *more*. Same with living in Linlithgow. It's alright, but it's no Glasgow or Edinburgh or London.'

'Aye, it's awright fur you – you've got qualifications an' that. You can get oot whenever it suits ye.'

'If I could get out whenever I wanted do you think I'd still be living with my parents, stacking those shelves?'

I fix him with a look. He glances at his shoes, then up as the old woman walks past clutching a white card in her hand.

'I suppose. Seems like we're aw fucked, eh?'

'We'll get out eventually, Niall.'

'Aye, wan way or another.'

He nods and I follow his gaze. The nurse is walking over to the row of chairs. Niall takes a deep breath and I glance over at the little girl, who is paused mid-song and looking at her mum. The nurse stops and checks her clipboard, the pen in her hand tapping an awkward beat against her palm. Eventually the beat stops and she looks back up at the row of patients and visitors.

'Niall Robertson?' she says.

12

Niall looks around as he walks through the doorway and I nod. He gives me a thumbs up but his face doesn't match the gesture. Then the door swings shut and I'm left in the waiting room. The little girl in the corner has gone back to her stories and her mother is sitting anxiously tapping her foot. The tapping seems to grow louder and louder until it's more like a gunshot every time she moves her shoe. Eventually she stops and stands up poker straight. She waits like that for a moment then walks over to her daughter. She crouches down, level with the little girl, and picks up a toy police car. She makes the siren sound and the little girl grins a gappy smile. She reaches out her little hands for the car and her mum hands it to her.

I look at the ground, understanding why so many people do in places like this. It's easier; less awkward than accidentally catching a mother memorising a moment with her daughter, or an old woman's tears as she leaves the ultrasound room. The floor is a faded blue colour, speckled with either glitter or dust – I can't tell. My heart is pounding. I don't know if I'm nervous for Niall's sake, or just because I'm in a hospital and this is where sick people die.

I pick up a magazine, determined to distract myself until Niall comes back, and open the pages randomly. I settle into the story and feel my stomach knot as I read.

That word – Cancer. Every parent's nightmare. I broke down in the doctor's office when he told me.

'What am I going to do?' I sobbed, as he patted my shoulder.

'We'll start treatment immediately,' he said.

'How will I tell my kids?'

I shut the magazine and stare blankly at the front cover. Shaking my head, I place the magazine back with the others and get up from my seat. I pad slowly around the room, looking at the posters stuck on the walls.

WASH YOUR HANDS

STOP SMOKING

FREE CONTRACEPTION

GET YOUR FLU JAB

I look at them each in turn, learning that alcohol handrub kills 99.9% of germs on your hands; the average smoker needs over five thousand cigarettes a year; you can get free emergency contraception from the NHS; and that the flu virus is constantly evolving so each year there's a completely new strain.

Hospital waiting rooms are really boring, but I'm thankful I'm not in the next room doing whatever Niall's doing, having whatever he's having done done to me. I check my phone. He's been in there fifteen minutes. It feels like a long time but then I don't know what the standard procedure is for examinations of any kind, never mind something that might be cancer.

I wonder what I would do if it was me. Would I have been brave enough to go to my GP and tell him 'I've found a lump'? Would I have been brave enough to get my balls out for the doctor to feel to confirm it? Would I have been brave enough to get the bus to Livingston and have another doctor scan my balls to see if it's life threatening?

I decide that yes, I would have been brave enough. I would have braced myself, like Niall, for the fight. I would have stood tall, chest puffed, and walked into the hospital ready to face whatever awaited me.

But then I realise that this isn't something that chose Niall over me. This is something that chose him and could still choose me. I glance down at my jeans. The button done up, the fly zipped to the top.

As I stand there, in front of the free contraception poster, I realise that in a very obvious way I really look up to Niall. It's easy to say I would do all of these things if I had to, but in real life – when you actually have that lump between forefinger and thumb; or you realise that you might just not have found it yet, or that it could still happen to you – actually facing up to it and making an appointment is probably an altogether different battle.

I slow my breathing, regain full control, and look at my phone again. It's now been half an hour since Niall went into that room. I walk back over to my seat and slump onto the hard plastic.

'Hellish wait, isn't it?' says the man next to me.

He looks like he's probably in his fifties. His face is tanned and weathered with a peppering of dark stubble across his cheek. A big, well-built man, I picture him on a building site. I murmur something noncommittal.

'Can I ask what you're in for?' he asks in his deep, scratchy voice.

'Nothing,' I say, not considering returning the question.

He nods slowly, as though thinking my answer through. After a second, he speaks again. 'Sorry for asking.'

The ultrasound room door opens and I bolt up from my seat. Niall walks out, murmuring thanks to the nurse, clutching a small white card. He's red in the face and shoots me a quick glance as we walk out of the waiting room.

Halfway down the corridor, Niall slows his pace and we walk beside each other. I try to think of something sensitive to say but the best I can come up with is, 'How was it?'

'Cold,' he says.

A silence builds before it bursts with the word.

'Cold?'

'Aye. That fuckin' gel they use. Freezin', man. Last place ye want it is yer fuckin' baws.'

I laugh and he cracks a smile. It's good to see him smiling again.

'So what did they actually do?' I ask. 'What happened?'

As we walk out through the hospital doors and into the car park, Niall tucks the card away into his jeans pocket.

'Well, I walked in there wi' that nurse, ken? An' she wis awright. Tried tae put me at ease. Telt me tae sit in this big chair-bed hing next tae aw this equipment, an' then she left. So I sat doon, hud a wee look aboot, jist waitin' fur the doc tae come in, y'know? Then, efter aboot five minutes or so, another woman walks in, smilin' at me the way nurses dae – that kindae pityin' smile. Anyways, I hink she's come in tae prep me or check the scannin' equipment or sumhin, so I'm like, 'Hiya', an' she sits doon an' says, 'Hello Niall'. So I'm thinkin' like 'Awright, how does she ken ma name?' an' *then* she says, 'My name's Michelle and I'll be doing your scan today.'

'Can you fuckin' believe that?' he says, eyes wide.

'Eh...' I don't really know what to say.

'The doctor in Lithgae didnae fuckin' tell me it'd be a woman doin' ma scan! So there's me jist expectin' another slightly uncomfortable experience with a male doctor fae the hospital an' instead I git a *brutally* uncomfortable experience wi' this *female* doctor. I tell ye, I wis no' prepared fur that.'

'But she's a professional, Niall. She was just there to do her job.'

'Aye, but even so. When ye've got a woman doon there, fiddlin' aboot wi' this fuckin' icy cold gel stuff ... Certain hings happen tae guys when it's cold, Ben, I'll remind ye ae that. Let's jist say I wis hardly feelin' ma maist impressive...'

105

I laugh and he does too. We reach the bus stop and balance on the seats.

'So, she comes in, you feel uncomfortable, she's not impressed. What else happened? You were in there for ages.'

'If ye want the gory details...' he says, scuffing his shoes against the ground.

'So she tells me how the machine works – sends waves intae yer body an' then they're reflected an' it makes a picture – an' warns me aboot the ice-gel. Then she puts on a pair ae rubber gloves, an' does that hing they do in Customs when they want tae search up inside ye, an' asks me tae unbutton ma jeans an' 'remove my underwear'. Luckily, this time, I'm no' wearin' ma fuckin' Superman boxers. Today I went fur a mair sophisticated look an' wore this classy pair fae George at Asda.

'So I'm sittin there, wi' ma jeans an' pants aroon ma ankles an' she's fiddlin' aboot wi' this machine, an' I'm hinkin tae masel *'The fuckin' situations you git yersel intae, Niall...'* Then she squeezes out the gel fur the scan an' rubs it between her fingers a wee bit – 'To warm it up a little', she says. An' I'm hinkin *'This is definitely the weirdest afternoon I've hud in a while'*. So she rubs the gel on an' it is BALTIC. Like puttin' yer baws in the freezer. An' she laughs an' says I'm pullin' a face an' I says back tae her, 'I bet you'd be pullin' a face if ye hud this fuckin' gel on yer bits'.'

I laugh and a bus drives past with LIVI YOUNG TEAM sprayed along the side. Niall's still laughing and he seems much livelier now, much more alive. I'm already doubting it's cancer just from how energetic he is. Cancer doesn't kill healthy people, I figure. This is a boy full of life.

'So she takes this wee scanner hing an' presses it against ma baws, lookin' aroon fur the ... y'know ... lump an' that ... An' she's watchin' the screen in case she spots it, so I look at the screen as well but I dinnae see anyhin 'cept a bunch ae grey an' black shapes. Then, efter fuckin' ages ae lookin', her haudin' the scanner, me haudin' ma dick oot the way, she goes, 'Ah, here we are'.'

'Did she tell you anything about it?' I ask.

'No' much. She said she couldnae tell me 100% 'cause she wants a second opinion, an' that she'd send pictures ae the scan an' a wee report aff tae some specialist. Said I should hear back in aboot a week.'

'That's really good – sounds like she's pretty convinced.'

'Aye, but there's still the chance, ken?'

'Yeah, of course, but if she'd been worried about it she probably would have done more; kept you in or something.'

'I suppose, aye.'

Niall glances up the road. There's a small group of people walking towards the bus stop and another bus – again, not ours – drives past with LYT sprayed on the back.

'Anyway, then she finishes the scan an' gives me a bunch ae tissues tae clean up wi'. She goes tae leave oot the staff door an' I say thanks an' aw that, 'cause she wis nice tae me, really calmed me doon. So she's left, an' there's me still lyin there on that chair-bed hing, frantically wipin' ma cock an' baws wi' tissues, an' wit happens? The staff door opens an' the fuckin' nurse fae earlier walks in, sees me totally rubbin' masel, covered in that gel.'

I'm laughing so hard my lungs hurt and Niall's trying to seem angry and outraged but I can tell he already finds it funny too.

'So I yell, 'cause I git a fright fae her bein' there, an' she goes 'OHMYGOD I'm so sorry!' an' turns her back 'til I get ma jeans on. Fuck knows wit she thought I wis daein'. I mean, in a hospital room? Who has a tug in a fuckin' hospital room?'

'So that's why you came out all red faced?' I ask, still laughing, tears in my eyes.

'Aye. That's why I practically fuckin' ran oot ae there. Scared she'd call security or sumhin! Fuckin' wankin' in a hospital bed, man...'

As we laugh, a group of lads a wee bit younger than us walk past, talking loudly. They're head to foot in tracksuits and trainers, their short hair gelled heavily like Niall's. They all have the same cocky swagger and as they get further away from us they start to chant 'LYT! LYT! LYT!' and swear at a police car that drives past. The car slows and the boys bolt, cutting across the hospital car park.

'Fuckin' hell, man,' Niall says, shaking his head. 'Wit is it wi' shitey towns bein' full ae total fannies?'

I laugh and look back at them. Now much further away, their chanting is a lot fainter, but I can still make out 'ON TOP! NON-STOP!' echoing down the street.

'Seriously, how d'ye fuckin' turn oot like that? It's folk like that that makes me really hink aboot Scotland – if it really is aw it's cracked up tae be, ken?'

'Is Scotland really cracked up to be anything?' I ask.

'Gid point,' Niall says, his laughter subsiding into a brief silence. 'I wis meanin' tae say, actually, eh, thanks fur coming along the day. I ken I said it earlier but I really mean it. It's pretty sound ae you tae help me wi' all ae this.'

'Ultra-sound,' I say, and he laughs and calls me a dick.

'Naw, really – you're a gid pal.'

We stand up as a bus turns the corner and slowly approaches. The doors hiss open and we get on and pay the driver. A grumpy, withered-looking man, he's wearing those glasses that reflect an image and as he says 'Right, ta,' and hands me my change, I realise it's the Saltire.

Niall picks seats at the back and we sit down as the bus swings out.

'So are you feeling better about this whole thing then?' I ask, as Niall gazes out of the window.

'So so, really. I'm tryin' no' tae hink aboot it anymair, but tae be honest, I'm still terrified. Aw I can hink aboot is c– ... y'know, the C word. I suppose the day went aboot as well as it could've though...'

'It's a battle won, anyway,' I say.

'Wan ae many,' Niall replies, looking out of the window again, his brow furrowed.

The bus judders as it swings on to the dual carriageway and the driver starts whistling loudly. Niall sings along, softly, to himself.

> *Oh, there were mony beating hearts*
> *And mony a hope and fear*
> *And mony were the pray'rs put up*
> *For the young Chevalier.*

13

The bus pulls in at the Cross, outside the Auld Hole, and we step off. Muttering thanks to the driver, I notice he's narrowing his eyes through the Saltire sunglasses at a group of school kids laughing loudly and eating Pot Noodles, dripping sauce over their polyester blazers.

'Oh, to be young again,' I say, and nod to Niall. He shakes his head.

'Nah, man, fuckin' hate they cunts. Too loud, too cocky, too 'individual' fur me. Teenagers should jist keep themselves tae themselves, ken? Sick ae these fuckin' weans hinkin they're sumhin special.'

'Aren't we all something special?' I ask in mock cheery-children's-TV-tone.

'Aye, but there's a difference between bein' special an' actin' like a fuckin' hyperactive 10 year-auld,' he says, eyeing them as they walk past and then snapping back to me. 'So, now we've toured the dazzlin' an' glamorous town ae Livingston, wit d'ye want tae dae now?'

'It's up to you,' I say, cautious of Niall's now barbed mood. 'I really don't mind.'

He looks left, then right, along the High Street, and then shrugs. 'Fuck aw tae dae in this place. Tesco fur juice?'

We walk to Tesco, Niall not saying much, me wondering what's going on in his head. I've been trying to determine his moods the whole way back from hospital. He seemed down, then fine – cheery, almost – and now flat again, bordering on angry. I try to think how I would feel in his position but all I can come up with is what Niall said earlier: cold.

'You alright?' I ask as we step into the warmth of Tesco.

'Always worried they'll ken I'm an Asda lad an' boot me oot,' Niall smiles briefly. 'Well, *wis* an Adsa lad.'

I don't say anything and Niall walks off towards the drinks cooler. I follow, remembering his outburst on the day the store got flooded.

The puddle.
The fall.
The argument.
'Paul, away an' fuck yersel'
Cans of food thrown on the floor.

'You wantin' anyhin?' Niall asks, tossing a bottle of Pepsi from hand to hand. I pick up a bottle of Coke. 'Posh twat.' He winks and I know he doesn't mean it. Or I hope he doesn't mean it.

We wander around the shop, Niall pointing out deals that are cheaper in Asda, products that aren't faced correctly on the shelves, and I realise he's spent so much time working there that it has literally become his whole life, his whole persona. Niall Robertson – Asda Boy. I wonder what he's going to do now he's lost his job; where to go from here?

'You're awfy quiet,' he says, and I blink back to the present. We're walking down the cereal aisle, Niall still tutting at the standards.

'It's almost like you were the wan gettin' his baws frozen off by a nurse who then caught ye havin' a chug intae a pile ae tissues.'

I laugh. 'Sorry, my mind was elsewhere.'

'Aye...?' he says.

'Doesn't matter – nothing interesting.'

'Compared tae wanderin' aboot Tesco in silence?' He stares at me.

'I was just thinking about working,' I say. 'Y'know, when everyone's, like, 9 years old, and they have a dream job, and then you get older and somehow all of those dreams fade away or get altered. It's just sad to think about all of those children who used to want to be the Prime Minister or a footballer or whatever, who, just because things didn't work out for them, had to make do with a job they hate. Sad to think we were all told we could be anything we wanted and then we grow up to find out we can't.'

Niall nods and I continue.

'Just when you mentioned there about how you used to be an Asda boy, I was thinking you could use this as an opportunity, rather than just unemployment.'

'How d'ye mean?' he asks as we turn into another aisle.

'Why not see this as your chance to get away from doing a job you don't like, rather than looking for another one?'

'Who says I didnae like Asda?' he says, and I feel my body tense, wary of crossing the line into patronising university student talking to a 'working lad'.

'Well, no one, but I just assumed...'

'It's tricky, ken?'

He pauses and I give him a look that says 'How so?'

'Take Jake an' Pete, right? They dinnae like their jobs. But they dinnae hate their jobs either. They jist ... exist wi' it, y'know? Like it's jist sumhin that hus tae be done, regardless. Everywan needs a job, an' that's theirs, end of. I never felt like that. I *liked* workin' fur Asda – I liked huvin' the responsibility an' maturity of huvin' a job, an' I liked belongin' tae a big company – that company – but I jist always thought that if I left I'd leave on ma ain terms, y'know? It's jist a bit ae a shock tae find yersel' so part ae somehin an' then tae huv it aw taken away fae ye. So yeah, I kindae dae like Asda, but then I'm also kindae angry aboot it.'

'Would you go back?' I ask.

'That depends on the terms. I'd go back tae work there now, aye, but I wouldnae stay there 'til I'm, like, thirty.'

'Aren't you worried you will though, by accident? Like how they say one day you wake up and you're forty – one day you wake up and you're a supervisor?'

'It's different fur you though. You've got a degree – you've got a chance tae get away fae all that wi' a clean slate. This *could* jist be temporary fur you. You've got so many mair options. My way out is by workin' ma way up an' then leavin fur sumhin similar, but elsewhere, y'know? Like movin' tae be a manager in a rival company or sumhin.'

He shakes his head. 'That's jist how it is fur me, an' fur Jake an' Pete. Fair enough, we might no' ever leave and become lawyers or rock stars, but dinnae put me doon as somewan who disnae huv any aspirations. Ye can still work a shite job an' huv a gid life, y'know? You're jist as much ae a person – a valid human being – as Johnny Gidjob, ken?'

I nod.

'Wit wis your childhood dream then, eh?'

I can feel my cheeks flush. 'I wanted to write children's books, like the Mr Men and Little Miss series.'

'Well that explains goin' tae uni tae study books, doesn't it?'

I laugh. 'Same sort of literature a lot of the time, I suppose. What was your dream?'

'I wanted tae be wan ae The Corries,' Niall says, somewhat proudly. This doesn't surprise me at all, Niall fancying himself as part of the most Scottish of Scottish bands. 'I even learned guitar so I could play their songs. I realised I'd niver be a Corrie, obviously, but it wis a nice feelin' when I wis wee; like by learnin' guitar I wis wan step closer tae singin' *Scotland Will Flourish* on stage at Murrayfield.'

'D'you still play?' I ask, imagining him in full Highland gear, flashing the crowd with one foot on a monitor.

'Aye, wee bits an' pieces. I wis in a band fur a while but now it's jist me in ma room, ken? I mean, we werenae that serious – jist covers an' that – but it wis a gid laugh while it lasted.'

'Ever thought about getting back into a band?'

'Ach naw...' he says, shaking his head.

'Why not? Might be a good earner – I've seen pubs here with house bands that get paid. That'd sort your Asda blues out.'

'Ah, it's jist a dream, ken? I'm nae Johnny Marr or James Dean Bradfield. I'm Niall Robertson – Asda Boy. I ken I said I've got aspirations, but bein' a rock star jist seems a bit farfetched, ken?'

We turn the corner and find ourselves walking down the Home aisle. Niall points at one of the shelves and I look at the label on the product.

LAVENDER REED DIFFUSER – AIDS CALM
AND RELAXATION

'Speakin' ae dreams,' Niall says, 'I bought wan ae them the other day, tae try an' help me sleep better.' He gives me a knowing look.

'Did it help?' I ask.

'No' really. I've been huvin' problems, tae tell ye the truth. Strugglin' tae sleep, wakin' up in the night, that sort ae hing. Nightmares. Man, these nightmares are fuckin' extreme. I've been wakin' up sweatin', pure fuckin' terrified. 'Aids calm and relaxation' my arse.'

'What are the nightmares about? Leaving Asda?'

Another knowing look from Niall, but darker this time. 'About the hospital. About ... y'know.'

'Ah, right.'

We walk in silence for a bit and then Niall speaks up.

'Like this wan dream I hud; it wis the first wan, an' I've hud it a few mair times since, worse each time. I'm sittin' in the hospital, right? In the radiology department, an' I'm in a hospital gown, with the crotch open an' ma baws oot. There's a nurse there an' she's bein really nice an' tryin tae reassure me aboot it aw, an' we're jist chattin' an' then she puts her gloves on an' gets oot the ultrasound cream. I laugh an' make a joke aboot how weird the situation is an' she laughs an' it's aw fine, but then the room seems tae get darker an' when I look doon my legs are strapped tae the chair by ma ankles. I try tae reach over an' undo the buckles on the straps but when I move my arms I realise they're strapped in tae. An' then I look over at the nurse an' she's still laughin' but it's, like, really scary laughter, an' she goes, 'This won't hurt a bit, Niall', an' starts rubbin' the cream aw over ma baws. Aw the time she's still laughin' an' when I look up where the ceiling should be there's jist a load ae folk lookin' doon on me – like, ma mum an' ma da, ma granparents, you boys fae work, man, it's everywan I've ever met – an' they watch me as the nurse pulls oot this rusty auld saw blade an' grabs haud ae ma baws. An' then right as she goes tae make the first cut, jist before the saw bites intae ma skin ... I wake up.'

'Fucking hell,' I say.

'That's no' even the worst wan.'

'Does it get worse than having a nurse saw your balls off?'

'There's this other dream – I huv it probably jist as much as the other wan, but wi' this wan I never wake up before the end, no matter how much I want tae.' He coughs then starts.

'So I'm lyin' on this huge double bed, the room's aw covered in candles an' there's this cheesy saxophone music playin in the background. An' I'm lyin' there wi' ma shirt off, torso rippling with muscles, lookin' like some kindae male model or sumhin. Aye, I'm lyin' there, lookin' aroon the room when the en-suite bathroom door opens a crack, an' this woman walks oot.'

'Sure this is the right dream you're telling me about here, Niall?' I ask.

He looks at me and I know to stop joking.

'So this woman comes oot, dressed in this sexy silk gown hing, soft curls in her hair, sultry eyes, ye ken the drill. She comes oot an' walks over tae the bed, climbs on, an' crawls across tae me. I'm still jist chillin', muscles-aplenty, enjoyin' the moment, an' she starts kissin' ma neck an' bitin' ma ear while her hand creeps down ma chest tae ma stomach, tae ma belt – undoes the belt, tae ma buttons – undoes the buttons, slips her hand inside...'

I feel myself blushing now and I can't see what Niall's expecting me to be horrified about except the fact that he's telling me a dirty story in the middle of Tesco.

'An' she moves her hand slowly across ma skin, an' her fingers feel light as feathers, sendin' shivers all up an' doon ma legs, ma back – makin' the hairs stand up on ma neck an' aw. An' then, right as her fingers go a bit lower, she stops an' pulls her hand oot. She gives me this look, like she's tryin tae dae a really hard maths puzzle, an' then apologises.'

'I don't get it,' I say.

He speaks again, only his voice sounds thin, breaking sometimes. 'She says, 'I'm sorry, I didn't realise you were only half a man', an' then gits up an' leaves. An' I look doon an' see ma jeans undone, a stiffie, an' wan lonely baw sittin' by itself. An' that's when I wake up. Half a man.'

Niall looks at me and I can't think what to say.

'An' tae be honest, that second dream frightens me mair than the first, 'cause I ken the first wan won't ever come true.'

'Niall, they're just dreams – it's just your mind playing out irrational fears. Irrational, Niall.'

'But wit if that's no' irrational? Wit if that's wit ma life is gonnae be like? If I do git bad news fae the doctor an' they operate an' by a miracle I survive but wi' only wan baw – if that's wit happens then that second dream could come true. Mair than jist the wance as well. I don't want tae spend the rest ae ma life alone 'cause I'm scared ae tellin' – showin' – any woman what I'm actually like. Half a fuckin' man.'

'You won't be half a man, Niall. And you don't even

know if they would have to operate to remove *it*, or if you even will have *it*. You said yourself the nurse was hopeful...'

'Aye, hopeful. There's folk supportin' Falkirk FC who're fuckin' hopeful – disnae ever mean they'll ever actually win the SPL.'

'Well, have they even given you any statistics? You're probably worrying about something which is really unlikely to happen,' I say, hoping what I'm saying is true.

'Aye, they gave me statistics. Listen tae this,' he clears his throat grandly, as though calling the store to attention. 'If it is the Big C then there's a 96% chance I'll survive.'

'Well that's amazi–'

'BUT,' he cuts me off, his voice loud, aggressive, 'if it is the Big C then there's no two ways aboot it: they WILL cut the whole hing oot – baw an' aw. 100%, no matter wit.' He stares at me. That same defiant look I've seen on him before. We stand still there in the aisle for a moment.

'Tae be honest, Ben,' he says, his voice different now, softer, 'I'm no' too sure I can cope wi' aw ae this. I'm beginning tae hink I'm losin' it a bit. Mood swings, no' sleepin' ... fuck, man, I flipped oot an' lost ma job, an' now I'm yellin' at the wan mate I've got, fur nae reason. Sorry. I'm sorry.'

'Don't worry about it, Niall. You'll be fine. Don't think about what might happen – just focus on what you know for certain right now. The doctors are hopeful which means you should be hopeful. They know their stuff.'

He sighs heavily. 'Aye,' he says, 'Aye, sorry, I'm jist freakin' oot, y'know? I hate aw this waitin'. I hate no' knowin' wit's goin' on doon there. Every time I see it aw I can hink is that it's like a ticking clock, jist waitin' 'til the right moment tae fuck everyhin up – well, mair so than already. There's a part ae me that jist wants tae cut it aff the night – dae it masel' right now an' get it over wi, y'know?'

'You just need to try and distract yourself. The doctors are happy to wait so it can't be *that* urgent. Try to unwind, get your head together, and like I said – use not being at Asda anymore as an opportunity to do what you really want to do.'

'Aye, I suppose,' he says as we walk towards the self-service tills.

'We need a day out – a proper one without hospitals – we could get Pete and Jake in on it too, if you fancy.'

Niall pulls a bit of a face, just for a moment, but I see it. He pushes a few twenty pence coins into the machine. 'Mibbe, aye. Might be gid jist tae git away fae here. I'm goin fuckin' crazy in this wee town, tae be honest.'

I look around Tesco, seeing all of Linlithgow squeezed into its small shell. 'Yeah, me too.'

Niall picks up his bottle and scrunches the receipt in the palm of his hand. I scan my bottle through and see Niall with his thinking face on. 'Aye, a wee day oot might be gid. Jist chill. De-stress. Aye, a wee quiet wan.'

14

Outside, a horn is beeping. My phone's buzzing on my bed but I'm too busy searching under piles of jeans and old t-shirts to answer it. Eventually, I find my wallet and grab my coat. Stuffing my phone into my pocket I run down the stairs and shout a goodbye to my parents. They're having a drink, engrossed in the tennis on the TV, and shout goodbyes after me. I slam the front door and run to the waiting car.

'Fucking hell, you take your time!' says Jake, already pulling away from the kerb.

'Sorry – couldn't find my wallet,' I say, before greeting Pete and Niall.

Pete says hi and Niall mumbles a hello while adjusting the CD player.

'Will you fucking leave that!' snaps Jake, batting Niall's hand away.

'S'no' ma fault you've git shite taste in music.'

'Here, this is *my* car–'

'This is your Mum's car, Jake,' Pete interrupts.

'This is *half* my car, so I pick the music. If yous don't like Warrant you can fucking walk.'

Niall sinks back into his seat and I fasten the belt across my chest.

'So then, boys,' starts Pete. 'Excited about a bit of *Trainspotting* today?'

He'd found it online – Falkirk Cineworld showing *Trainspotting* for one week only, as well as *Gregory's Girl* and *Braveheart*. It was meant to be a celebration of all things Scottish but *Trainspotting* hardly seems like a celebration, more a brutal display.

'It's no' aboot celebratin' the heroin an' deid babies, ya twat,' Niall had argued. 'It's because *Trainspottin'* is wit put Scotland oan the map as somewhere where folk *can* actually make sumhin decent ae theirself. The guy that wrote it got fuckin' minted affae it, an' it's aboot celebratin' that. No' fuckin' heroin, fuck's sake. Heroin looks shite.'

'Great film,' says Jake, driving us down over the Canal bridge.

We all start quoting classic lines, dissolving into laughter after each one. But right as I bring out that one about heroin beating any fucking cock in the world, the car falls silent. I look round, desperate for someone to say the next quote but all eyes are fixed outside the left of the car.

'That was a quote, guys, I wasn't–'

'Aye, we know, Ben,' says Pete as Jake slows to a halt and winds the window down.

'Excuse me, bud,' he shouts, turning the CD player off.

A policeman walks over slowly, as if his legs are so heavy he can hardly move them. I recognise him vaguely and see the scene in my mind.

The policeman watching me drag Niall from the wall, shaking his head like a disappointed parent. You've not let me down; you've let yourself down.

He crouches at the window and Jake speaks across Niall, who is slumped in his chair, flicking through Jake's CDs, muttering *pish, pish, pish, nae bad, pish, pish, pish.*

'What happened here?' Jake says.

I lean around his seat and look out of the windscreen. The whole road in front of us is cordoned off and there are blue lights flashing EMERGENCY EMERGENCY.

'There was an accident at the station this morning, so all the adjacent roads are closed – you'll have to turn back and head towards the Academy.' He points behind us.

'An accident? Like, a train crash?' Jake asks.

The policeman stares at Jake for a second and then says, 'There's a woman been hit by a train. Now will ye's turn around, please?'

Jake puts the car in reverse and swings it round. Winding up his window, he turns his head slightly. 'I'm losing count of how many people have done themselves in at that station,' he says.

'There was one the day I moved back through,' I say. 'Some guy stepped in front of a rush hour train. Burst him apart.'

'Fucking hell...' Jake mumbles, flicking the CD player back on.

'It's like suicide central in this town,' Pete says, absently tapping on his iPhone.

We speed down Royal Terrace, alongside the rail line, and cut back onto the High Street. I look out of the window and watch the street flit past. The take-aways, the pubs, The West Port.

I found a wee lump.
I found sumhin, Ben. In the shower. About a week
ago.

The song fades out and the CD plays the next track. A rolling beat on the snare drum fills the car. Jake taps his fingers on the steering wheel.

'All a-fuckin'-board!' the singer howls, as a guitar revs into action. Jake turns it up and soon we're proper boy racers – roaring across town, blaring music with our windows down. Jake sings along, his fingers beating the rhythm harder on the wheel.

He gets about two lines in before he realises he's singing along to a song about catching a freight train out of a small town towards the big city. Niall suddenly punches the off button and the car falls silent. I bite my lip, shooting Pete a 'Fuck, that's bad' look. Pete looks away.

'Petrol,' Jake says quietly, indicating into the Murco garage. 'Back in a sec.'

We pull up and Jake gets out, slamming the door behind him

'Fuckin' hell,' laughs Niall. 'Awkward...'

Niall and I talk about *Trainspotting* for a bit, while

Pete taps away on his phone. Niall's explaining that, 'Princes Street jist isnae the same unless ye've git *Lust Fur Life* blaring in yer ears. Ye do that wee run doon Calton Road, a bunch ae CDs in yer jacket ... magic', when Pete waves for our attention.

'Here we go – look, we're on the news,' he says, holding out his iPhone.

A local news website shows the headline 'DEATH AT RAIL STATION'. Underneath there's a photograph of a woman sitting smiling on a beach and a short paragraph surrounded by adverts for Visit Scotland souvenirs and Gumtree listings. I vaguely recognise the woman but can't quite place her. In wee towns like Linlithgow, mind you, everyone recognises everyone to some extent. I take the phone from Pete and read the article.

RAIL services between Edinburgh and Glasgow have been suspended after a woman was struck and killed by a train at Linlithgow station this morning.

A spokesperson for British Transport police said the woman has been identified as local Judie Easton, 46. They are not treating the death as suspicious and her family have been informed.

'Hardly dizzying levels of fame, is it?' I say.

Niall scrambles round, chucking Jake's CDs into the footwell of the car.

'Gies a look.'

I pass him the phone and look out at the garage. Jake's walking back across the forecourt, tucking his wallet into his back pocket.

126

'You alright, Niall?' Pete asks.

Niall's gone really pale and his hands are shaking.

'Niall?' Pete says again, waving a hand in front of the phone.

'She fuckin' did it,' Niall whispers.

'What?' I say.

'She fuckin' did it. She fuckin' killt hersel'.'

'What are you talking about?' Pete asks, an edge in his voice.

Jake opens the door and gets in, his mood improved from earlier.

'That woman I yelled at the other day in work,' Niall continues. 'I telt her tae fuck off an' kill hersel' ... an' she fuckin' has.'

The woman's face clicks into place: standing at the till, tears rolling down her face as Niall rants and storms off; Paul walking her to the office, apologising, offering tea and discounts; her, walking out of the shop, eyes fixed on the floor, sniffling. Her stepping out in front of a rush hour train, the driver sounding the horn before the metal rips through her flesh and bones, sending pieces of her scattering amongst the commuters, across the car park, down to the High Street, and up into nearby trees.

I look up at Niall but he's shrunk back into his seat and is staring out of the passenger window.

'It's not your fault, Niall,' I say. 'I was there – she was ... *damaged*. Probably would have done it anyway. What are the chances? ... Y'know?'

I'm not even sure if I'm lying. She was a bit strange but she hardly seemed on the edge. People on the edge probably wouldn't leave the house to shop in Asda, I think. But then again I work in Asda and I constantly feel on the fucking edge.

A horn sounds behind us and Jake moves the car back on to the road. He turns left and heads back into Linlithgow.

'Where are we going?' Pete asks. 'What about *Trainspotting*? Choose Life and all that.'

'Pete, fuck's sake,' I say.

'We're not going to the fucking cinema anymore,' Jake says, eyes fixed on the road, Niall still slumped next to him. 'I can't be fucked with all that lowest of the low, scum of the earth shite. We, boys, are going to blow off some fucking steam.'

'What d'you mean?' I ask.

Jake looks in the rear view mirror, his eyes lit up with life, energy, the hint of a plan.

'I happened to get, when I was in the garage, a wee text from a certain young lady named Chloe...' He over-pronounces her name and smiles as my ears – no doubt literally – prick up.

'And she said, if we haven't anything better to do, that we should come round to her flat for a party.' He pauses and lets the words sink in. 'Of course, I said no, because we were going off to watch a film about skag addicts and shoplifters, but given the fucking depressive mood in here–' he spits the last words, 'I thought it'd be better if we all sit back and get as drunk as we possibly can, eh?'

Niall sits up in his seat and looks at Jake.

'Jake, I'm no' really up fur a perty. I mean, jist think how I'm feelin' now.'

'I have thought, Niall,' Jake replies. 'You're miserable and there's no point in wallowing in it. That's what they *Trainspotting* guys did and it didn't really get them anywhere, did it?'

Pete points out that Renton makes 'about 14 grand' in the film but Jake tells him to fuck off.

'Naw, I'm no' really in the mood, ken? I appreciate it but I jist can't. That fuckin' woman...' He shakes his head and looks out of the window. 'That fuckin' woman...'

We sit in silence, Jake steering us through the streets slowly. The mood of the car is undecided, tense, unsure. We stop at a set of traffic lights. Jake turns to Niall and then looks back to me and Pete. 'Right, decide now, lads. We turn right for the party or straight on for Falkirk.'

It feels like a life-changing decision.

'I'm easy either way,' I say, trying to will the wheels to turn right.

Pete shrugs. 'It's not really up to me, is it?'

After a pause, Niall says 'S'no' ma fault. Is it, lads?'

We all say, 'No, of course not, how could it be?' and Niall's mood seems to lift. He's clearly wavering about the party and eventually asks if Chloe said anything else.

'She said it'd just be her and a few of her mates...' Jake smiles as the lights change to green and cars behind us beep their horns.

'I suppose maybe a wee perty wi' a few lassies might help, aye,' says Niall, and Jake grins.

The car pulls up outside a small shop with metal grills on the window. We all run inside, trying to avoid the heavy downpour. Inside, the shop is dark and smells sickly sweet. An old woman watches us from behind the till, sucking her teeth. We walk over to the alcohol section and I browse. Niall's already procured himself a 70cl of vodka and a bottle of Irn Bru, waiting for the rest of us. Pete picks up a bottle of vodka half the size of Niall's and walks off towards the mixers, as Jake selects an orange bottle with a black label saying MD 20/20. I collect six cans of lager and walk over to the till.

One by one, we buy our drink from the gawking, teeth-sucking woman. She gruffly asks me for ID, having ignored the others, and studies it carefully. Grunting, she hands me a blue bag and we run out to the car. Niall's studying Jake's drink, perplexed.

'Jake, how come ye've bought this pish?'

'Just a laugh, you know? All the wee mental neds drink MD, so I thought it'd be funny.'

'But you're no' a wee mental ned. Drinkin' this jist makes ye look like a prick,' Niall says.

'Right-oh, Niall. D'you want some haggis with your Irn Bru?'

'Fuck off,' he shoots back. 'Made fae girders, like me. Solid as fuckin' steel. Cannie beat vodka an' Bru. An' anyway, I need sumhin strong tae take ma mind affae hings.' He looks at me and I glance away.

'Yeah, I know,' Jake says.

'Naw, ye don't,' Niall replies.

Jake eyeballs back, shakes his head, and pulls the car back out onto the road. We speed back past the pubs, the yellow-lit windows blurring into streaks in the rain. Jake turns on the CD player, swapping the disc. A different 80s band this time, but the same songs about dirty glamour and love. Jake sings along, banging his hands on the wheel, as Niall says, 'I suppose sum ae this 80s music isnae *too* bad...'

The atmosphere in the car changes. Totally changes: as if Niall had never spoken to that woman, or she'd decided not to take that last step off the platform. It's electric. I feel an energy crackling through all of us. Niall opens Jake's MD and takes a swig.

'It's actually no' bad, this,' he says, eyeing it like a fine wine in a fancy restaurant.

He offers it round and Jake doesn't mind. We're tearing along the road, past Sainsbury's and onto Mill Road, and I know each of the guys in the car feels exactly the same as me – *untouchable*. Nothing seems to matter anymore: not the biblical rain outside, or Niall getting fired, or the dead woman's body parts scattered across town, because we're young and driving fast and on our way to get drunk. This is really living. Jake cranks up the music, the speakers rattling from the bass.

'Tonight, boys,' he says, yelling over the music, 'we are getting fucking hammered!'

15

We slow to a stop outside a series of garages next to a small shop on the corner. Describing itself as a 'General Store', it's really just a shop that used to sideline selling tools and milk with selling alcohol to school kids. I remember seeing huge packs of them come out of there, with rucksacks and Academy ties on, carrying blue bags full of cider, vodka and alcopops.

We get out and as I swing the door shut I see a woman standing at the door of the shop. Dripping wet, with hands full of reeds and algae, she's watching us. The car doors slam in unison and I blink. There's a small Indian woman watching us with her arms crossed, before flipping the sign on the door to 'Closed' and walking back inside the shop. I look at Niall to see if he noticed but he's busy talking to Jake about Duran Duran's *Wild Boys*.

'So, d'ye hink they wur sayin' that aw boys are jist like animals in human bodies? Like, we aw huv a wild side tae us?'

Jake shrugs and locks the car. 'I dunno. I figured it was about being young and not having anything to do and I guess that brings out the animal in a lot of people.'

'Aye ... aye,' Niall says thoughtfully. 'I niver kent Duran Duran wur that deep.'

'Where are we headed, Jake?' Pete asks, looking around, his eyes squinting against the rain. 'I've never been to this end of town before.'

'Cause there's fuck aw here,' mutters Niall.

Jake looks around, his phone to his ear. 'Hello? Hi, Chloe? It's Jake. Yeah, yeah, we had a change of plan, so we decided to come. Listen, we're in Avon Drive right now – whereabouts is your flat?'

We stand in silence, looking around for the girls at a window, or opening a front door. My hair drips water onto down my collar and the cold makes me shiver.

'Yeah? Okay, be there in a sec.' Jake flashes a grin and points at one of the flats above the garages. 'That's us, boys. Door's round the other side.'

We walk round, bottles and cans rustling in plastic bags, Pete telling me he 'quite liked that wee Hannah but Jake seemed in there...' with a disheartened shrug. I reassure him that there are other fish in the sea, possibly even this little pool we're entering tonight, and that he shouldn't be too put out. It seems odd to have Pete talk to me like this, like a friend, but then again, everything feels different tonight. The world has changed and it is ours.

We clink to a stop outside a white front door with a dirty, frosted glass window. Jake rings the bell but there's no sound, so he knocks. A moment later, the door swings open to reveal Chloe smiling at us. Smiling at me.

'Hi guys, come on in,' she says, gesturing behind her.

We walk in to a small hallway and collect awkwardly. The hall is plain: chipped magnolia walls and no photographs. For some reason I was expecting hundreds of holiday photos or pictures from classic nights out. There are four doors leading off from the hallway; the door to the bathroom is ajar, as is one leading to a bedroom. I peer in as Chloe leads us to the kitchen/living room and catch a glimpse of a full length mirror, a CD player, clothes everywhere (shoes, tops, jeans ... bras) and a bed. A double bed with white sheets and black cushions on top. Cushions I can see myself knocking aside as Chloe and I, drunk with lust and lager fall into the room and–

–trip on the threshold. I stumble into Jake, who turns and steadies me, glaring.

'You alright, Ben?' he asks, the tone in his voice suggesting that even if I am, I soon won't be.

I laugh awkwardly, stutter a reply and look around. Hannah is sitting on a sofa across the room, giggling; a glass of gin/vodka/water in front of her. In an ashtray by her drink there's a fat, homemade cigarette trailing sweet coils of exotic smoke. I'm sure the others must have clocked the weed but then again they're maybe too busy wishing they hadn't brought the boy with the clown feet to the party.

My cheeks flush as I take a seat on the second, vacant couch. Niall sits next to me, chuckling, having procured a glass from somewhere, and starts combining his Irn Bru and vodka in a mix I'm sure could blind a horse. I think of a TV show I used to watch when I was younger;

Bernard's Watch, where a young boy could stop time with a pocket watch. I wish I had one of those. I would rewind it and stroll into the room, looking suave, wink hello to Hannah and fall onto the couch with an arm casually draped around Chloe.

Instead, I sit quietly as Hannah turns on the TV, a generic chart music channel, and starts talking to Pete. She takes a drag of the joint and exhales slowly, the smoke clouding around Pete's head like a lion's mane. Niall's sinking into his drink, his face braced so as to hide the vodka wince, and Jake asks Chloe about the party.

'Oh, there'll be some more people along later,' she says, smiling. 'I just thought we'd get things started a bit earlier, y'know?'

Jake smiles back and says 'Yeah, I know what you mean' with a look in his eyes I don't like. I crack a can of lager and drink deeply. The lukewarm bubbles fill my stomach and I instantly feel more relaxed. I look for a way to ease myself into Chloe and Jake's conversation.

'So, how many of your friends are you expecting?' Jake asks.

Chloe pauses for a moment, counting. 'About three or four.'

'But don't worry,' she continues, noticing Jake's expression, 'they're all great. They really know how to get a party going.'

Jake sips his MD from the bottle and smiles, a bead of orange falling down his chin. Chloe laughs as Jake realises. He wipes his mouth with his hand, turning away slightly. I smile, not sure if dribbling your drink is on the same level as tripping over, but I feel like we're even now.

'So,' Chloe says, her eyes locking with mine, 'how do you boys feel about a drinking game to get things going?'

All I can think is that good things will happen if I say yes. I take a deep swig and finish my beer.

'I think that sounds fucking perfect,' I say, crumpling the can in my hand. I feel like Danny Zuko crossed with The Fonz. I am literally the coolest thing on the planet at this moment. Tonight, I decide, will make up for everything bad that's ever happened.

Chloe leaves the room for a moment and then comes back with a bowl, a pack of cards, and a bottle of Tequila. Hannah, now sitting next to Pete, shakes her head at Chloe.

'No way. That game fucking destroys me,' she says, laughing. 'Remember the last time? I was so drunk I fell down the stairs, threw up and then passed out in it.'

Chloe laughs, sets the bowl down and says, 'I know. It's going to be great fun.'

Niall shuffles forward and sets his vodka and Irn Bru down on the table. 'So, wit are the rules? I'm no' playin' sumhin wi' *tons* ae rules.'

Chloe takes a deep breath. 'It's simple: you draw a card, if your card is anything from two to ten you drink three fingers of your drink, Ace means you do a shot, Jack means you down your drink, Queen means you make someone pour their drink into this bowl, King means you pour your own drink into the bowl, and Joker means you remove an item of clothing...'

Her eyes flick to me briefly and I smile. Niall shuffles forward even further.

'Remove an item ae clothin'?' he says.

Chloe nods.

'This sounds like a fuckin' dangerous game, ladies...'

Pete winks at me. He mouths 'You were right' and then says loudly, 'I'm in – let's get this started!'

I think to myself that maybe this is it: this is the moment I really crack the concrete facade of Pete and he finally accepts me as one of his own kind; as well as being the moment Chloe declares her undying lust for me. If it's a choice between the two though, I figure I don't really need another guy friend anyway.

Chloe sits down and we gather round the table. Hannah's turned the television up and over her shoulder a woman is dancing in a bikini while a looping bassline fills the room. She hands the joint to Pete, who takes two deep drags before passing it to me.

We take turns drawing cards and before long the bowl is half-full, Jake's lost his t-shirt and I've done two shots. I look around the room, feeling hazy and warm. I'm nearly finished my beers now too. Pete's vodka and coke mix is almost gone, Niall's still got about half of his 70cl left, and most of Jake's MD is either in the bowl or his stomach. The girls are sitting together, fresh joints in their hands, drinks on the table. Smoke billows and my vision blurrs as I watch Chloe and Hannah. The room darkens slightly and as they speak into one another's ears, the music and storm outside grow so loud I can't hear what they are saying. I can't hear anything except the distant rumble of thunder and the thudding pulse of last week's number one single. I reach out and steady myself on the couch. Balance gone, I reach to take a fresh joint from Niall, who's grinning at me: Cheshire Cat in a smokey flat.

The smoke burns my lungs but I breathe deeper, sucking the joint hard until my eyes water. I exhale and feel weightless and heavy all at the same time. Coughing out a laugh, I look at Hannah and Chloe, ignoring the drunken rabble of the boys around me. The girls are whispering secret things to each other and then the room tints with green light from the TV and it's all very atmospheric and Shakespearean. A storm on the muir outside, witches conjouring at their cauldron.

I laugh, trying to remember the plot of that play. *Hamlet*? *Othello*? No, I think. It's something closer to home ... The Scottish Play. It floods back to me and I rest my head on the couch from the weight of thinking. And then, in a tartan accent, I recite in my head:

Life's but a walking shadow, a poor player
That struts and frets his hour upon the stage,
And then is heard no more. It is a tale
Told by an idiot, full of sound and fury,
Signifying nothing.

I laugh louder this time. Niall looks over to me, still grinning, his face wide open.

'What's so funny?' he asks, his voice slow and low, like a record on the wrong speed.

Chloe and Hannah are looking at me as well and I can't seem to stop laughing. 'The Scottish Play,' I say, tears dripping down my cheekbones.

The room is spinning and I hear myself cackling '*Macbeth, Macbeth, Macbeth*' before the room lightens and I settle. I sit for a while, gazing into the centre of the room, letting the very real wave of drunkenness and stonedness and loud music wash over me. My mind fills with the **thump thump thump** of the bass drum and *chick chick chick* of the hi hat, and Dizzee Rascal starts rapping about getting away from the same old shit you're tired of. I wonder why the TV is playing *Holiday* since it came out years ago and then I get up, stumbling out to the bathroom.

The guys cheer as I walk off, shouting 'Three finger forfeit' and 'Wanker', and I bump from wall to wall until my outstretched hands reach the cold enamel sink and I lock the door and just try to breathe

b r e a t h e

b r e a t h e

I lean against the tiled wall for a moment, looking at myself in the mirror. I try to fix my hair, make sure my shirt is sitting right, check my teeth, and decide that actually, I look quite good considering how messy I feel. I take another few deep breaths. As I feel everything fall back into place there's a BANG BANG BANG on the door. A few more follow and the door handle turns and rattles. I flip the lock and the door swings open. Jake runs in, still shirtless, his hand over his mouth. He pushes me aside, lifts the toilet seat, and sprays vomit into the bowl.

His hands are grasping the side tightly, his knuckles white as he heaves wave after wave out of his mouth. Niall and Pete appear, cheering like they're at a football match.

'Waaaaaaay!' Niall shouts, pointing at Jake's hunched figure.

Pete's laughing hard. 'What a fucking lightweight.'

'He seemed fine when I left,' I say. 'What happened?'

'He drank the bowl,' says Niall. 'Aw his MD, ma voddy, your lager, an' aboot six shots ae Tequila fur gid luck. Plus he's been puffin' they joints like a fuckin' steam train.'

Jake's still pumping vomit into the toilet. I close the door behind me and we stumble back into the living room. Hannah's flicking through the music channels on the TV again and Chloe's on the phone.

'Yeah ... yeah, cool. That sounds perfect. Oh don't worry; we won't be leaving anytime soon.' She ends the call and looks up. 'Is he alright?'

'Yeah, he's fine. Just heaving his guts up in the toilet. He'll be right as rain in a wee while,' Pete says, slurring his words, slumping down onto the couch.

Chloe stands up and turns to Hannah. 'I'm going to go check he's not ruining our bathroom. You keep this lot entertained.'

Hannah laughs and points at the bowl. 'Shall we try round two?'

Niall moans and shakes his head like a spoilt child before picking up his Irn Bru bottle and topping it up with more vodka. My mind feels clearer now, slightly, but my body still feels numb; tingly with drugs and alcohol. I crack my last beer and sip it slowly, listening to the music from the TV. Another dance song that I half-recognise yet have probably never heard before. I tap along to the beat on my beer can.

'Ye ken wit I hate?' Niall says loudly.

Pete sighs and says, 'No, Niall. What do you hate?'

'Aw this *shite*.'

'All what shite?' I ask, taking another sip.

'Aw this shite ye git wi' modern life. Aw this *work* an' *school* an' *college* an' *pensions* shite.'

Pete nods silently.

'Jist hink – before the Age Ae Modern Man, none ae this shit existeed. Mankind wis a simple race. If we wur hungry we'd go an' eat. If we needed a pish we'd go an' pish. None ae these cavemen hud tae deal wi' *mortgages* an' *bank loans* an' aw that. Nuthin' cost money. An' that's how I hink it should be now. A simpler time. I want the whole wurld tae git back tae a simpler time, wi' tractors an' that.'

He pauses and looks around. Pete's still nodding and Hannah's listening intently.

'Honestly – an' I can say this withoot feelin' like a wanker – but I'd love tae huv ma ain farm. I'd love tae live affae my ain farm an' no' huv tae deal wi' aw the pish an' shite the rest ae the world heaps on itsel'. I'd be totally self-sufficient.'

I take another sip and stand up, stumbling slightly. No one pays any attention and Niall keeps talking. 'See that wuman who killt hersel? Imagine how she'd huv felt if she could huv escaped it aw an' lived on a wee farm. I hink she would huv felt a lot fuckin' calmer, happier. See, Pete...' He grabs Pete's arm and motions to Hannah. 'Here, I've kent Pete fur years. *YEARS*. An' he'll tell ye I'm a down tae earth kindae guy. Sure, we huv oor differences, but that's wit makes the world go roond, eh? See, I dinnae want much oot ae life, do I, Pete?'

I turn to walk away as Pete shakes his head.

'I jist want tae be a happy guy. Nae stress, jist happiness; that's wit I say.'

I look back at them to see Hannah looking at Niall and Pete, a bemused look on her face, and then I leave Niall to explain Life.

The hallway is quiet except for the muffled sound of the dance songs coming from the TV. I walk towards the bathroom and see the door is still shut. I'm walking in a fairly straight line, though it's taking some effort, and I stop and grab hold of the door handle. It turns smoothly and I push the door open. Jake's still over the toilet, now spitting and cursing tequila.

'You alright?' I ask, looking over my shoulder for Chloe.

'Getting there,' Jake says, still spitting.

He looks up at me. His long fringe is streaked with vomit and it's smeared all down his chest as well. The smell hits me full on and I take a step backwards so I'm standing on the threshold.

'I just came to check on you. Have you seen Chloe?'

'Chloe Chloe Chloe,' he says. 'She's lovely. Fit as. So's Hannah.' His face freezes and he looks suddenly terrified. 'Do they think I'm a total prick for throwing up?'

I hesitate. 'No, don't worry. They thought it was ... funny.' I look around again. 'Right, I'll leave you to it.'

Jake hangs his head again and I shut the door behind me. I walk back along the hallway, one arm pressed against the wall to keep me steady, and pause outside one of the bedroom doors. I can hear Chloe talking to someone.

'Yeah, just let yourselves in. No, no idea at all. Yeah, right, see you soon.'

I knock on the door and then push it open slightly. Chloe's sitting on her bed and I feel suddenly unsteady. Time slows and when I speak my voice sounds different, like it's not my own.

'Hi, Chloe, d'you mind if I come in?'

'Not at all. Come have a seat,' she says, tucking her phone into the pocket in her jeans. 'How's Jake?'

'Better. He's just sorting himself before he comes back out.'

'Good stuff. That was my mates. They'll be here soon.'

She smiles and I can't stop looking at her smile, her teeth, *her lips*.

'I'll tell you something,' she continues, 'you're a hard man to track down. That number you gave me wasn't recognised so I had to get Jake's off Hannah's phone. I was worried I'd never be able to get you here.'

There's a flash in her eyes; electric, exciting.

'Can I tell you something?' I say.

She nods.

'I feel like there's something here. Something between us,' I say, my mouth moving, making these words come out as my brain screams 'Stop! You'll fuck this up!'

'I feel like since we met there's been a kind of ... *connection* between us. I've never really believed in fate or anything like that, but there must have been something that made me move here, that made you come over to us in the club, that made you invite us here ... something that made you come and sit on your bed ... something that made me join you...'

She looks at the bed, her hand stroking the duvet. She bites her lip and moves closer. 'Well, Ben, maybe there was something that attracted me to you, something that made me invite you boys here, something that made me leave the room and wait for you here...'

She smiles that smile again and my whole body feels electric.

'Maybe something is going to happen tonight ... Maybe,' she pauses, 'you'll have to wait 'til later to find out what it is though. Maybe you'll just have to be patient.'

She takes my hand and stands up. My heart is beating so hard I'm scared I'll break ribs. She leans in close. So close I can feel her warm breath against my lips. So close I can smell her perfume. I'm unsteady on my feet but her grip on me is solid.

'Good things come to those who wait, Ben,' she whispers, a smile dancing across her lips.

She pulls on my arm and walks past, leading me back to the living room, where Jake is now sitting by himself, his t-shirt on backwards. Niall's still ranting and now Pete is involved too, arguing that 'Life is for fucking living, not working'. Hannah looks up at us and Chloe winks at her. She smiles and turns the TV off so that when Niall says, 'Wit is it aboot some Scottish folk that jist makes them so fuckin' rough an' scummy?' he says it too loud and looks embarrassed for a moment. We sit down and Niall continues, lowering his voice.

'I mean, dinnae git me wrong here, I love Scotland. Everywan kens that. I'm proud tae say I'm Scottish, but I've come tae a conclusion recently, ladies and gentlemen. Here goes ... Sometimes I jist fuckin' *hate* the people here. I hink, aw in aw, it's the people of Scotland that let Scotland doon, tae be honest. Now, I'm no' sayin' everywan, but some folk seem tae almost revel in the fact that this country hus a bad side. Folk who act like 'cause they live in a rough area it's a gid hing. Tae be honest, I'd rather we jist fixed up aw ae the rough areas, y'know? Rather than playin' intae that fuckin' stereotype ae violent drunken Scottish bastards, we should try tae show the rest ae the wurld that we're actually decent, clever, civilised human beings. I mean, hink aboot it: we, as the Scottish nation, huv it pretty sweet. We've got free education, free healthcare, free prescriptions, a ton ae oil everycunt's efter, the best whisky in the world ... I mean, we even invented the fuckin' TV! So it really fuckin' grates on me when ye git these folk who are just ... shite, when by aw rights we should aw be pretty well aff, ken?

'See, I hink – an' this is probably mair relevant now than ever – if we're gontae be a strong, independent nation, we need tae shape up a wee bit. I mean, dinnae git me wrang here, Scotland's no worse than maist other places, but it's also no better, eh? I'm fine wi' admittin' that Scotland right now needs a bit ae work, but we need tae git the people tae actually do that fuckin' work. I mean, some ae us are puttin' the work in, aye – Scotland hus plenty ae gid books, gid films, gid music comin' ootae it – but it's the general public who jist arenae makin' a fuckin' effort. Example: I lost ma job, but I'm no' jist givin' up. I'm lookin' everywhere, ken? Jack ae aw trades, me. Things are gonnae work oot – mibbe no' themorra, mibbe no' the day efter, but wan day. I jist ken.'

Jake's applauding and I'm laughing with Chloe and imagining kissing her here, right in front of everyone, and I don't know where all this confidence has come from; it's maybe the lager or it's maybe that feeling I had in the car that we're untouchable because we're young and drunk and stoned and stupid and happy, but either way, that's the image I have in my mind as the living room door opens and a group of three guys walk in.

We all look up in unison, still laughing and, for once, happily agreeing with what Niall just said, until we realise that we know the guys who've just walked in and the laughter stops.

16

'Awright lads?' The guy in the middle steps forward. 'Huvin' a wee perty, I see.'

I look at Niall; frozen solid, drink in hand. Pete's leaning forward, looking at the floor, muttering 'fuckfuckfuckfuckfuckfuckfuck'. Jake is dumbstruck, his eyes no doubt fixed on the cricket bats held by the two at the sides. I look at Hannah, who is smiling at the boys, and then to Chloe, but she gets up and walks over to them.

'What the fuck?' I say, still looking around.

The room is blurry and I feel underwater. I can't tell if this is real or if it's the drink and the weed making me hallucinate. Chloe walks away from me. The guy speaking, the guy with the knife from that night in the Auld Hole, lets her merge into him. Her arm loops around his back and his round hers. He looks at her and winks. She grins.

'Chloe...' I say.

'Don't say a fuckin' word, dickhead,' the boy with the bat nearest me says.

I shut my mouth and sink into the couch, praying it

will swallow me up and spit me out back in my room, Falkirk, Neverland, anywhere.

'It's been a while since we hud a wee meet up, isn't it, lads?' the middle one continues. 'Last time I remember we went for a midnight jog aroon the Peel, didn't we?'

Pete shifts. 'Guys, let's just calm this down a bit,' he says.

'I'm totally calm.' The boy squeezes Chloe's waist. 'I'm fuckin' settled. It's mibbe you lads who need tae calm doon.'

And then I see it, underneath Chloe's arm as it snakes around his thick waist. A dull, dark shape sticking out from the waistband of his joggies. There's a flash of lightning and again the room seems to spin, and now I'm sitting in the Auld Hole in the Wall, listening to Niall talk about pride and honour and all that and

'Here!' One of them shouts again, taking a step forward, 'wan ae you boys pulled a blade on me last week.'

He reaches inside his jacket pocket and pulls out a small kitchen knife. Smiling, he turns it slowly in his hand.

'Well now it's ma turn.'

I feel totally separate from what's happening in the room right now, until a soft voice pulls me back to the couch and the lads and the girls.

'Ben.' I look up and Chloe's looking at me. Her face seems different. I hardly recognise her. 'I said stop fucking staring at me.'

I keep looking, my mouth sitting useless and empty. She laughs and it cuts through me.

'What did you expect, Ben? That'd I'd kiss you? Fuck you? Fall in love with you?'

The rain gets heavier and there's another flash of lightning.

'Aww, did he take a wee fancy tae you?' The knife boy walks over to me, his voice thick with sarcasm, leaving Chloe standing with the others. 'Did you huv a crush on ma wee Chloe there? Did ye hink she'd invite ye tae hur flat an' it'd be aw romantic an' candles an' that?'

The image floats across my mind for a moment and then a low grumble from the sky outside bats it away.

'Stupid boys,' Chloe laughs. 'Always thinking with their dicks and not their heads.'

The boy's hand moves to the back of his joggies. My head throbs and sweat seeps from my pores. He sneers and whispers, 'I could sort that oot right now.'

He pulls out the knife and holds it against the crotch of my jeans. I try to look to Pete or Niall or Jake for help but the other lads have moved to the middle of the room, bats held up, ready.

'Wan wee *flick* an' that'd be you,' he says.

'Eddie, no,' Chloe says and I look over to her, eyes filled with gratitude.

She's going to save me, I think. *She'll talk them down.*

'Not like that,' she says, walking over.

Eddie moves to the side, letting Chloe stand in front of me. She looks beautiful and I feel stupid for still thinking that. She looks me up and down, curls her fist and slams it into the side of my head.

She hits hard and I know it's probably not the first time she's done it. My head throbs and the figures in front of me blur. I rub my temple gently. Chloe spits and the wetness sprays across my cheek and lips. Half an hour ago I was dying to taste her saliva but now it just stings as she hits me again, bursting my lip. I taste blood and as I run my tongue across my teeth I feel a wobble. Chloe turns her back to me and walks out of the room.

'Yous planned this,' Niall says, still drunk enough to slur his words. 'In Code. Yous came over an' ... yous hud this aw planned oot.'

'Smarter than you'd think, huh?' says Hannah. 'Course we'd planned it. You boys are an easy group to spot, especially in a wee shitehole like Code.'

'You see, lads, efter oor wee *confrontation* in the Auld Hole we didnae hink that oot an' oot violence wis the answer. We wanted sumhin a bit smarter; a bit mair ingenious,' says Eddie, now pacing around the room like a movie villain.

'Y'see, Mikey here,' he nods at the skinny boy holding a bat in front of Jake and Niall, 'proposed a *friendly chat* efter you boys finished work some time. Figured a car park at night is as gid a place as any. But we thought there's still sumhin better than that. Sumhin that's no' jist gontae be a gid *place* tae dae this but a gid *way* tae dae this.'

He laughs, the kitchen knife resting in his right hand.

'An tae be honest, when Hannah suggested this, I did hink it'd be gid, but so far this has been fuckin' hysterical.' He laughs again, pointing at me. 'You, greetin', bein aw 'Chloe, I thought ye loved me' an' the rest ae yer mates quietly pishin' theirselves 'cause they ken there's only wan way oot ae here an' it's that   fucking door.'

He waves the knife towards the living room door and I hear Pete sigh another series of fuckfuckfuckfuckfuckfuckfuck's.

'So wit d'yous want tae dae thenight?' Eddie grins. 'I thought we'd mibbe huv a bit ae Question an' Answer.'

'Fuck off, Eddie,' Niall shouts.

In an instant, Eddie's across the room and his fist is slamming into Niall's head. His face red with anger as Niall cowers, trying to curl up like a hedgehog. Eddie's yelling, striking on every word.

'DON'T   YOU   TELL   ME   TAE FUCKIN'   FUCK   OFF'

He punches one more time then steps back, his chest puffing in and out, white spit on his lips. He wipes his mouth with his hand and glares at Jake and Pete.

'Either ae yous want tae fuckin' speak up?'

They stare back at Eddie and say nothing.

'Gid.'

I look over at Pete, willing him to come up with another brilliant escape. I flash back to the Auld Hole and Pete picking up his pint glass, throwing it at the lads, us running, jumping walls, tearing through overgrown bushes, running running running until we burst onto the bus, throw money at the driver and fly off to safety like the Millennium Falcon bursting through hyperspace. Instead, Pete looks back at me, terrified, and I realise then, with another flash of lightning, that there is no clear way out of this. Even cement-solid Pete is shitting himself.

Eddie is stalking round the room, staring at each of us, as the two other boys – Mikey and a bigger guy whose name I don't know – stand guard with their cricket bats, ready to relieve us of our consciousness/brains/kneecaps. I don't know where Chloe's gone and for some reason I feel much more on edge because of this. Hannah's still loitering by the door, now watching us with a blank look.

'Not exactly exciting, this, is it?' she says.

Eddie turns to her, eyes wide like he's on something, and glares. 'Too fuckin' bad. We're jist gettin' started here. Jist you wait an' see. Things'll liven up.'

She sighs heavily and turns, walking out of the room.

'Well, now it's jist us lads, eh?' Eddie says, sitting on the table, facing me. 'So let's huv some lad chat. Ben, I see you've taken a wee fancy tae ma girlfriend. Is that right?'

I stare at the ground, my head still throbbing from where Chloe's fist hit me. My teeth still wobble when I run my tongue across them.

'Is that right, Ben?' he says again, his voice more edgy.

I stay silent. Eddie grabs me by the throat, his fingers digging deep into my windpipe.

'I thought she seemed nice, yeah,' I cough.

He swings his fist round in a wide arc and brings it smashing into my skull.

The room moves like waves, then dulls to shadows followed by flickering brightness. A warm red stream flows down my face. My hearing is thick and distorted as Eddie screams

YOU CANNAE FUCKIN' HUV HER.

SHE'S MINE

SHE'S   MINE

FUCKIN'   BELONGS

                              TAE

ME
OKAY?
And as my eyes cloud I see him drop the remains of Niall's glass on the floor, the bottom jutting upwards in jagged shards, the rest still in my skull like a crown
                              of
                         thorns.

My eyes flicker open and I'm lying on the couch. Concentrating on my pulse, I count the throbs, trying to work out if this is what bleeding to death feels like. Pulse after pulse growing weaker, maybe; it's hard to tell. At the other end of the couch, Pete's slumped backwards, his eye a deep blue and purple, a large red welt on the side of his face. Mikey's standing over him with the cricket bat, his face half-proud, half-scared of what he's done.

I turn my head and the pain sears across my skull. I close my eyes and grimace, before opening them again to see where Niall and Jake are. In my head, they're fending off Eddie and the other guy like two Saint Georges, spearing dragons with MD bottles and kitchen knives, but when I look over I see Jake lying on the ground, Eddie's friend kicking him over and over in the chest, face and stomach. Jake's vomiting over the carpet with each boot and then the guy stamps hard on his face, smattering his shoes in puke.

Backing into the corner, Niall's trying to stand to his full height and look intimidating. He's too drunk though, and stumbles into the TV, knocking it over with a loud bang and a crackle of electricity.

'I've been waitin' fur this moment, ye ken that?' Eddie says, 'When it's jist you an' me, wan on wan, nae mates or anyhin.'

Niall's shaking and I try to sit up. My arms are jelly and I collapse back into a heap each time I try.

'Definitely no' the hard man now, are we? Backin' up, greetin', beggin' fur me no' tae...'

I push myself up again, focusing all my energy, trying to shake off the concussion. Mikey's turned his back on Pete, who's lying unconscious next to me, and is helping his mate kick Jake in the kidneys. I look around but the room is tilting every time I move. It feels like a fairground ride gone horribly wrong and my stomach turns and clenches like I'm on the waltzers. I manage to stand up and stumble a few steps towards Eddie, who's still threatening Niall.

'EDDIE!' I shout, my voice hard and determined though my legs aren't.

Eddie and his mates turn towards me. My knees bend and I pounce towards him, fist raised high. My mind is whirring. Thoughts spilling through the thick fog as it dissipates. This is Mercutio vs Tybalt, Hamlet vs Laertes, Every Great Hero vs Every Great Villain. I feel triumphant – valiant – alive.

Then, as my fist collides with Eddie's cheekbone, something in my head clicks and I remember the conclusion to the Shakespeare plays I studied at uni.

Mercutio gets stabbed.

Hamlet gets stabbed.

The hero doesn't always win.

I bring my arm back for another blow but Eddie beats me to it. His iron-solid fist hammers into my face. Something cracks and my legs buckle. I fall to the floor, limp and empty. Fists and boots pummelling down onto me as they beat the breath from my lungs, the acid from my stomach and the thoughts from my head.

I look up and see that it isn't Eddie, Mikey or the other boy; they've cornered Niall, advancing like hyenas on Simba. Instead, Hannah and Chloe are punching and stamping on me, Hannah spitting insults, Chloe laughing harder with each blow. Flashes of blue, green, red, yellow.

A scream rings out and Niall falls crumpled to the floor, blood gushing from his face.

For a second I think they've stabbed him, but when Chloe lifts her foot I see the knife lying underneath the couch. It must have fallen out when Eddie hit me. I try to reach out for it. Chloe's shoe comes down on my hand and I scream as something inside splinters. I bring my hand back, close into my chest, and try to curl up as small as possible.

Still the kicks come down and my head is   aching, blood   trickling.   The   room
fades.
Fades
until all I can see is a tiny hole in the darkness,
a pinprick image.
Niall's face,
eyes wide,
mouthing something I can't make out.
The hole disappears
and all I'm left with is a voice
above me,
distant and echoing,
like God or an angel
speaking
to a dying patient in a hospital bed,
saying
'Right,
let's get these dicks oot ae here.'

17

I was faced with a thousand choices. The Careers Officer had asked me what I wanted to be when I was older and I told her I didn't know.

'No idea at all?' she sighed.

I shook my head.

She told me I had good grades so far but that my choices for Standard Grade make a huge impact on my future.

'For example,' she said, her voice smooth, 'if you choose to drop Biology you'll struggle getting into medicine, whereas dropping Geography will have little effect there.'

I told her I didn't want to drop Biology because it's the easiest science, never mind anything about medicine, and that Geography had never been my strong point. She asked me what my favourite subject was.

'English,' I said.

'Well then, Ben, I suggest you may be look into a future there. For now, why not consider keeping your options open – English is compulsory, remember, as well as Maths and French. How about the three sciences;

history, which I see you're doing well in; and...' she trailed off, studying the papers on her desk.

I looked around her room. It was tiny, with a motivational poster on each wall. The one on the back of the door said KEEP CALM AND CARRY ON in huge letters. She probably put that up more for the students than herself, and I wondered how stressed I would be when it was my turn to sit the exams.

'...you can pick the last one,' she said, finishing our meeting with a smile.

At home that night, I talked to my parents about the choices.

'She said I should keep my options open until I can decide what I want to do for a living.'

Dad chewed his dinner with big determined movements; his teeth grinding into the chicken flesh so loud I could hear it from across the table.

'Well,' he said, swallowing, 'I agree with her. You shouldn't drop important subjects without knowing what you want to do with your life. You don't want to throw away opportunities at such an early stage.'

Mum nodded, picking at the food on her plate.

'I don't want my son turning out like some drop-out with no options. In a gang or dealing drugs, you know?' he resumed. 'I think it's admirable when you have a young person who knows what they want from life, and so they pursue it. Who's that boy...?'

He waved his fork towards Mum. She looked up at him, waiting for a further clue.

'The one who fixed the Roberston's bathroom after that cowboy–'

'Oh, I know who you mean,' she said, the name on the tip of her tongue. 'Ah ... oh, what's he called?'

'Never mind,' Dad continued. 'Him. He was, what, about 19, 20? Left school at 16, got himself an apprenticeship and now look at him: earning more than most of the people living in this street, myself included! You see, I think that's brilliant. It just goes to show you don't need to go to university to do well; all you need is some sort of direction, drive, and ambition. I won't have you throwing your life away to work the first job you can find, drowning your sorrows every Friday night, fighting in the street like those louts down by the takeaways.'

He sipped his wine and stared hard at me.

'You just give it some thought – find out what you want to do with your life and then go after it. Everyone can make something of themselves if they try hard enough. Regardless of what it is, if it's what you want to do, and you put the work in, I'll be proud. Plumber, manager, teacher, doctor, whatever.'

'Just take your time,' Mum said, smiling at me in a pitying sort of way. 'I'm sure you'll do what's best.'

White, dazzling light burns across my eyes. My head feels cracked, like the sun is boiling everything inside. I look around. The sky burns blue and empty. The storm has gone. The ground beneath me is still wet, though, and my clothes are soaked through. My fingers twitch and I feel damp grass brush across my skin. I manage to stand up, legs shaking like a newborn fawn.

I lower my gaze from the sky. I'm standing by the roadside in a patch of long, wild, uncut grass. My eyes sweep across the green and I spot a dark lump a few feet away from me. I walk over. Raising one hand to my head, I feel dry, crusty blood in my hair. Last night comes spinning back to me.

Eddie smashing a glass on my head. Chloe and Hannah kicking and punching me until...

Until what? There's nothing more after that last image; Chloe's foot stamping on my head. Nothing more. *The rest is silence.* I can't even remember who said that.

I reach the shape in the grass. It's a body, lying face down, sprawled out like a starfish. I reach out to touch its t-shirt and feel a sharp pain shoot through my palm. My fingers are gnarled and bloody, sitting at awkward angles. Chloe's foot, her whole weight snapping my fingers as I reached for that knife.

I look back to the body, notice the t-shirt is on inside out. I crouch slowly, feeling the blood rush around my head, making me feel faint, and then reach out with my good hand to turn it over.

Jake, splattered in blood and vomit. His skin is bruised and cut. My stomach tightens and I throw up in the grass. I spit a few times and wipe my mouth on my sleeve. I don't know what to do. I check my pockets for my phone but I can't find it. My wallet's gone as well. I look around the street for help but there's no one around.

Jake's eyelids flicker and open. He looks at me, unfocused, and then slowly shakes his head.

'Jake?' I say, whispering. 'Jake, are you okay?'

He studies my face for a moment. 'Ben,' he says. 'Fuck ... what happened to your teeth?'

I move my tongue around my mouth, feeling the enamel of my back teeth before reaching jagged edges and a hole at the front.

'Fuck,' I say, running a finger around the inside of my mouth. 'Is it bad?'

He nods. 'What happened last night?'

'No idea. I don't remember anything except getting a fucking kicking,' I say.

'Where are Niall and Pete?'

I look around but can't see them. The street is still and it has that silent, eerie tension like a horror film.

'Can you stand?' I ask.

He pushes himself up and I grab his arm to help. He looks at my other hand, hanging broken and useless at my side.

'What do we do now?' he says quietly.

'We need to find them.'

'D'you think they'll be okay?'

I walk back to the flat. The curtains are shut and I stand facing the door while Jake catches up.

'What you doing?' he hisses.

I rest my hand on the doorknob, take a deep breath and turn it. Jake inhales sharply as the handle jams and the door doesn't move.

'It's locked.'

'Good,' Jake glares. 'Fuck were you wanting back in there for anyway?'

'What if Niall and Pete are still there?' I say.

Jake's face falls. 'Fuck,' he says.

We stand in silence for a moment, wondering what to do next.

'Let's keep looking for now. There's nothing we can do if they're still in there,' Jake says, his eyes lingering on the doorknob. 'With them...'

We walk back along the path, towards the road.

'How do you feel now?' I ask.

'Better. Still a bit woozy, but better. My chest is fucking killing me though.'

'They were proper laying into you back there. Really gunning for your kidneys.'

'I don't remember,' he says softly, looking at the ground as we walk.

'It was brutal,' I say.

'What about you? How's your hand?'

I examine it, turning it gently back and forth. 'Fucked. She really went to town on it.'

'It looks totally crippled,' Jake says.

'Feels it. My head's aching too. That Eddie cracked a glass on me.'

'Jesus ... They were animals.'

'I know. That'll teach me for fancying someone's girlfriend.'

Jake chuckles but wraps his arms around his ribs as the pain smarts.

'I thought she seemed nice,' I continue. 'Turns out she was a total maniac.'

'I think we all got played, Ben. Totally fell for it, hook, line and sinker.'

'Makes you wonder, doesn't it?' I say.

'What?'

'About guys. Men.'

'What d'you mean?'

'That we pretty much rule the world but we're so easy to manipulate.'

Jake laughs, again clutching his ribs, muttering 'Fuck's sake.' 'Easily led, we are,' he says.

'Look!' I say, stopping and pointing across the road.

Jake follows my gaze and squints. 'Is that–?'

'Niall's shoe.'

We walk over and I pick up the shoe. It's still wet and there's a smear of red across the white material. I hold it out to Jake but he's not paying attention.

'Found them,' he says, pointing down an alleyway to our right.

At the far end, there are two figures. One sitting on the ground, his back against the side of the alley with his leg outstretched; the other sitting alongside, head in his hands.

'NIALL!' Jake shouts.

I grab his arm. 'Shh!' I hiss, nodding towards the flat. 'What if that lot hear?'

'Shit, sorry,' he says.

Niall's hands are clutching his extended leg and his

face is puffy and pale. He squints his eyes as we approach and then nudges Pete.

'Fucking hell!' Pete says, 'Where have you two been?'

'We woke up just round from that flat,' I say. 'What about you?'

'We were out that way and round a bit,' he points out of the alley. 'Tried to look for you but Niall's leg's fucked so we had to stop.'

'Broken, we hink,' Niall says, his teeth gritted. 'That fuckin' Mikey stamped on ma knee an' sumhin must ae snapped. Last hing I mind.'

Pete nods at my hand.

'What happened to you?'

'Chloe's right foot,' I say. 'Broken as well. What about your face?'

He runs his fingers over the huge red welt on his face, which blends into a vicious-looking black eye.

'Lucky nothing's broken. He hit me with that bat like he was going for a fucking home run. Still dizzy when I stand though, and my ears are ringing like fuck.'

'Fuckin' hell,' Niall says, shaking his head. 'They fair went tae town on us, boys.'

I sit down next to him. Jake joins me, easing himself down gently, swearing under his breath. We all sit there for what feels like years, just breathing, feeling, thinking. Every now and again one of us whispers a string of swear words as we move whatever body part is injured.

The sun rises higher in the sky and it becomes apparent that it's still very early in the morning. None of us have our phones or watches, so we're not sure exactly, but Pete guesses around four or five in the morning. Jake asks 'What are we gonna do?' three times, met with silence, before getting an answer.

'We're gonna go home and rest. Fucking heal up,' says Pete. 'Get ourselves back to normal.'

'And then what?' Jake asks.

'I've seen that boy Mikey before, working in Poundland in Falkirk. We could wait outside the Howgate Centre and follow him after work one night. Chloe and Hannah live just there, obviously, so Eddie will be easy enough to get–'

'Woah, woah, woah,' I say, raising my unbroken hand. 'Are you saying we try and get them back for this?'

'What did you think we were gonna do? Just let it slide?'

I stare at him, amazed. 'Well yeah! I figured, given the fucking hammering we got just there, that we should leave it. They've won. End of.'

'They've only won if we let them win. If we got them, one by one, they'd be fucking terrified.' Pete turns to Jake. 'What d'you reckon? Sound like a plan?'

'I'm not letting them away with this,' Jake says, jaw steeled. 'Imagine how that'd look. They'll be telling everyone we just took a beating. What if someone else has a go?'

'We did just take a fuckin' beatin',' says Niall, his voice tense. 'We took a fuckin' firm beatin' an' this happened,' he waves his arms, including us all in a wide circle. 'I'm no' wantin' tae 'git 'em back' 'cause I'm no' wantin ma other leg tae fuckin' match this piece ae shite.' He exhales loudly, shaking his head. Jake and Pete are glaring at us both now.

'What's going to happen if we jump each of them then? D'you think it's going to stop there?' I ask.

'Depends how bad they get left off,' Pete says firmly.

'Worse than us now?' I ask. 'I've got a broken hand, Jake's probably got cracked ribs and Niall can't even fucking walk. It doesn't get much worse than this!'

'That's what you think,' he says darkly.

I almost laugh. 'Pete, this isn't fucking *Kill Bill*. You can't win here. It's over.'

'Pete, d'ye no' want oot ae this?' Niall says.

'How? How can we get out of this?'

'I dunno, like, move away or jist fuckin' stop aw this fuckin' violence.'

'Move away?' Pete laughs. He looks almost like a different person now, though I can't tell if that's just the swelling around his eye or something else. 'How the fuck do you expect me to afford to move away? And stop the violence?! Are you having a fucking laugh? Do you think I wanted this? If you remember correctly, Niall, this is all your fault!'

'Ma fault?! How the fuck did ye figure that? It wis Jake that brought us here. I wis aw up fur watchin *Trainspottin'* yesterday!'

'I'm not talking about who drove us here, fuck's sake, Niall. I'm talking about who pulled a fucking knife on

Eddie one night in the Lithgae Arms. If you hadn't played the fucking hard man we wouldn't have been in this mess in the first place.'

Pete glares at him but Niall doesn't break his gaze.

'Aye, well it's done now,' Niall says, 'But if you hink I'm aboot tae walk back intae that flat an' take another beatin you can fuck right off.'

'Fuck's sake, Niall,' Pete spits. 'There was me thinking you would always back me up. Time after time I've looked out for you, put up with you, and now this. What happened to you? You're like someone else now.'

'Pete, just leave it, yeah?' I say as he stumbles to his feet. 'We can get out of this. We don't need to get sucked down to their level. Rise above, y'know? Move on.'

'And you? Who even are you? Fuck off, mate. You and that fucking Chloe girl ... You know how I got this?' He points at his bruised eye, now swollen shut.

I stand up but don't say anything.

'I got this because when Eddie fucking glassed you I tried to jump in. I tried to defend you and got a fucking cricket bat to the head for my trouble. I shouldn't have bothered, University Boy. You and this dick can fuck off to your 'better lives' and see how far you get.'

I turn to Jake, ready to talk him down, to stop him leaving with Pete, but he beats me to it.

'Ben, don't even bother. You know, I always reckoned you thought you were better than us. Better than 'just' stacking shelves. Well you know what? Look at yourself. You went to your university and got some shitty

167

meaningless degree and look where it got you. Right back here with the rest of us, slogging it out, week in, week out, 'til we can afford to get our own flat somewhere and work another shit job.' He prods a finger firmly in my chest, 'But you know the big difference between you and us? We don't think we're better than anybody. And that counts for a lot.'

He pushes past me and just I stand there, mouth agape, and watch him and Pete walk off.

'Aye, well fuck yous both!' Niall calls after them.

Jake gives us the finger as they disappear around the corner.

'Eh, d'ye mind stickin' aboot?' Niall says.

'Course,' I say, sitting down next to him.

'I dinnae hink you're a prick, if that's any consolation.'

'Thanks, Niall,' I say.

'An' I agree with you, by the way. Aboot tryin' tae break oot ae this cycle, this fuckin' town. I'm sick ae it. I dinnae want tae be fifty, still stackin' shelves wi' a bunch ae teenagers. I dinnae want tae be the guy still goin tae fuckin' Code at the age ae fourty fuckin' four. I dinnae want tae be wan ae they guys who's worked in the same shop all ae his life, gone tae the same clubs, done aw the same old shit, but hasnae got anywhere. Tae tell ye the truth...' he lowers his voice to a whisper and leans over, half-smiling. 'I hink I'm better than this an' aw. I hink maist folk are.'

'Yeah?' I say, and he winks.

'Aye. I mean, maist folk hink us shop workers jist exist in the shop, like, the shop front is aw they ken. They dinnae realise that we huv dreams an' goals an' aw that; hobbies an' passions. They dinnae realise that none ae us choose this life.' He shifts his hips, grimacing from the movement in his leg.

'Well, what do you want to do?' I ask.

'Honestly?' He says, pausing for a moment. 'Fuck knows.'

We both laugh and the pain in my head flares.

'But I dae ken sumhin – I want oot ae this, an' I hink that's enough fur me. You, you've git the chance tae really make sumhin ae yersel. You could be, like, a teacher, y'know? Sumwan that makes a difference. I dunno wit I could be, but I ken it's no' jist a replen assistant.'

'You know what I think you'd be good at?' I say.

'Talkin' the back wheels affae a Corsa?'

'Tourism. Or politics.'

'How?' he laughs.

'Because you have a real passion for, well, *Scotland*. God knows, you fucking live and breathe it. I think you'd be really good working for someone like Historic Scotland or the Parliament, y'know?'

'Aye, but I'd need qualifications fur that,' he says, sceptically.

'Well, aye, but you could maybe begin at the bottom and work up. Or why don't you think about college? There's one in Livingston, or you could go to Glasgow.'

'I dunno,' he says, and I can see his eyes tracing around the very concept of Glasgow – escape to the big city. 'Sounds like a total long-term plan,' he continues. 'I want somehin tae change, like, tomorrow.'

'You could do an accelerated course? Although Historic Scotland might just take you on, if you read up on your Scottish history – start by showing people around Stirling Castle, then work up into admin. That sort of thing.'

'Y'hink?'

Niall scrunches his face with thought.

'Worth a shot,' I say.

'Ken wit, Ben? Why no', eh? 'Bout time I bit the bullet an' started makin' ma way oot ae here. Fuck knows I dinnae want tae end up doin' aw ae that jist tae end up workin' at Linlithgow Palace. I hink we should make a pact. I hink we should promise each other tae dae oor best tae git oot ae this town, separate or thegither, regardless. Wit d'ye hink?'

'I'd say that sounds like a fair deal.'

We shake hands and hear the distant rumble of a car approaching.

'What about Jake and Pete? D'you really think they'll try and get back at Eddie and that lot?'

'Fuck knows, man. Tae be honest, I dinnae really care. I'll be happy if I niver huv tae set foot in this town again, niver mind deal wi' aw the fuckin' people.'

Somewhere nearby, a car door slams and Niall tries to push himself up slightly. He winces suddenly and grabs his leg. 'Fuckin' hell, wit did they dae tae me?!'

'That reminds me, have you heard back from the doctor yet? Y'know, about the, eh ... lump?'

Niall sighs. 'I've got an appointment next week, actually. Though it looks like I'll be spendin maist ae ma time seein fuckin' doctors now.'

'How d'you mean?' I ask.

'If it wis gid news, they'd ae telt me by now, wouldn't they? If it's bad news ... they'll want me in.'

I glance at his leg and then back up at him. His eyes are trained on the sky, staring hard.

'Remember, I'll come with you, if you want.'

He takes a deep breath. I feel something welling up inside me; a twinge of pity in my gut.

'Naw. Cheers, but naw, I'll be awright. I'm no' goin' tae face that fuckin' gang again, but I can face this.'

His chest puffs and for that moment, he actually looks a lot stronger. Then, as he exhales, the scared, beaten look returns to his face.

'Here!' A voice calls down the alleyway and we both turn to look, squinting against the glare from the sun. 'You lads alright?'

For a second, I think I see the woman from the loch, dripping wet, smiling, but I blink and she's gone: replaced. Now, standing at the other end, in gleaming uniform like a doctor or a nurse, is a postman.

'Actually, mate, no. Can you give us a hand?' I shout down.

He walks towards us, stuffing a pile of letters into his bag.

'What in God's name happened to you two?' he says, lifting Niall by one shoulder while I get the other.

'We had a bit of a, eh, *misunderstanding* with a group of old friends.'

'Jesus...' he says.

'Aye, but ye shouldae seen the state ae them,' Niall laughs, winking, then wincing.

'Oh, I see,' says the postman. 'Give them a good seeing to, eh?'

Niall grits his teeth as we move him, but still manages to squeeze out a sentence. 'Well, I hope I'll no' be seein' them again, let's jist say that!'

We sit down on a small brown bench by the main road, gently positioning Niall so his leg isn't at an angle, and the postman rings an ambulance on his mobile. He paces slowly behind us, reciting the street name in an over-pronounced, almost English accent.

'How d'you feel?' I say, turning to Niall.

He's staring up at the sky, watching a bird dip and soar through the morning air.

'Hm? Ye ken wit?' He glances back up at the sky, a smile playing across his face. 'I feel like a weight's been kindae lifted aff ma shoulders, ken? I feel quite optimistic.'

The bird flies in a large, elegant loop, before gliding off out towards the River Avon.

'Tae put it simply, Ben, all things considered, right now I'm actually feelin' pretty fuckin' gid.'

172

18

The ambulance stops at the bus stop in front of us and I'm disappointed we don't warrant sirens and lights. The postman nods as the doors to the ambulance open and a man and woman step out.

'Well, lads, I suppose I can leave you in their capable hands. Get on the mend, now,' he says, hoisting his bag onto his shoulder as he stands.

'Eh, thanks, by the way,' I say and he smiles before striding off, greeting the paramedics as he walks past.

'Ah, here we go,' Niall exhales. 'Next stop thigh-high cast.'

'You never know,' I say, 'you might get lucky.'

'Aye, I'm renowned fur ma gid fortune.' He laughs, then inhales sharply, clutching his knee.

'Woah, easy there,' says a man's voice.

The male paramedic is standing over us and the sun's glare around his head makes him look like Jesus in a painting. I squint past him and see the woman carrying a stretcher over towards us.

'Well then, boys, what can we do for you today?' she calls.

They're both about the same height, and bulky – that happy sort of weight that seems comforting. Their bright uniforms shine almost as much as the sunlight but the sting in my eyes is welcome. *We're going to be okay*, I think.

'Uhm, well, his leg's fucked and my hand's a bit of a mess,' I say, holding it out.

'Right, let's have a look here.' The man gently takes my hand and peers at it.

'What's your name?' he says.

'Ben. And this here's Niall.' I nod sideways and Niall attempts a smile.

'Pleased to meet you both,' says the woman. 'I'm Agnes and he's John.'

She continues to speak to Niall, asking where hurts the most and checking his pupils.

'So d'you mind telling us what led to this then?' says the man, still holding my hand up.

I hesitate and he smiles before I can speak.

'Ah, I get it. Fell over, eh?' he winks and I look at Niall. 'Well, at first look I'd say you've broken a few bones here, Ben, but an x-ray will clear that up. Anywhere else hurting? Your face looks like it might need checking.'

'Yeah,' I say, 'bit of a headache...'

He kneels down, level with me and I can smell his aftershave. It's a soft, warm smell – not the sharp alcohol like a lot of perfumes.

'Bad bruising...' he says to himself or me. I'm not sure. 'A few cuts and scrapes ... I'd say you took a pretty heavy blow to the head, Ben. Are you feeling any dizziness or sickness?'

'Sometimes,' I say.

He nods and holds a finger up in front of me. My eyes cross trying to focus on it and my vision blurs slightly. He moves his finger left, then right, and then up and down. I try my best to follow but he's frowning so I guess I'm not doing a very good job.

'Right, Ben, I think you have a concussion so we're definitely going to need to get you scanned.'

I nod and he tells me to try and keep my head still. Next to me, Niall is getting his leg strapped and Agnes starts to help him to his feet. John asks if she needs a hand but she shakes her head.

'Stronger than I look, John,' she winks. 'And so's this one. No need for the stretcher, actually.'

She moves slowly as Niall limps next to her, hissing in pain with every step.

'Your mate Niall's leg looks like it could be quite serious so it's probably best if we take you both in,' John says, picking up the stretcher.

'I didn't have much planned today, to be honest,' I say.

He laughs and his eyes flick across my face. 'With a shiner like that I don't imagine you'll have much of a social life for a while, son.'

'Is it bad?' I ask, raising my good hand to my cheekbone.

'Well, put it this way, with that eye and those teeth you

won't be pulling any girls soon.' He makes a consolatory face and I look at the ground.

'I don't think I want to get involved with any girl for a while, to be honest,' I say, my mind racing back to last night, Chloe's twisted face above me before she slams her foot down on my head.

John doesn't say anything. He just nods at the waiting ambulance and offers his arm as I get up. We walk over and I climb into the back where Niall and Agnes are.

'Full speed ahead,' John says from the front seat.

'Gonnae put the lights on?' Niall says, 'It's no' often I'm in wan ae these.'

John shakes his head and laughs as we pull away, speeding towards Livingston. Niall frowns like a sad child until John blasts the sirens for a moment.

'Fuckin' magic, that,' Niall grins. 'I'd huv that on aw the time if I drove this hing.'

We blitz along the road, the ambulance soaring over every bump and peak until we join the motorway, where John slows slightly to weave in and out of the traffic.

'Drives like a boyracer, our John,' says Agnes, winking at Niall. 'Never grew up past 17.'

'Nae point in huvin' aw they flashin lights if ye cannae take advantage,' Niall says. 'Must be a fun job, cutting aboot in this hing.'

'It has its downsides though,' Agnes says.

'Like huvin' tae come pick up handsome boys wi' broken legs?'

Agnes laughs heartily and pats Niall on the shoulder. 'Oh, no, son, you're one of the perks.'

They both laugh and I'm amazed at how relaxed Niall seems, given the state of his leg, his redundancy, his doctor's appointment next week. I look at the equipment in the ambulance, imagining how many people have sat where I'm sitting now, where Niall is sitting. How many people have lain on the stretcher, blood pumping from knife-wounds inflicted in silly pub arguments.

'Ladies and gentlemen,' John calls from the front, 'the next and final stop will be St John's Hospital, Livingston. That's St John's Hospital, the next and final stop. All passengers should keep hold of their tickets as barriers are in operation at this station.'

'Och, John, still dreaming of being a train conductor?' Agnes says.

'Sir Topham Hatt, the Fat Controller – my childhood hero,' John says. 'One of these days...'

The ambulance pulls up and we climb out, Niall being assisted by Agnes, who bats off his request for her phone number with a laugh.

'You're too young for me, Niall, and my husband wouldn't be too pleased!'

He winks at her and she laughs, calling him a right charmer. The main doors hiss open and John waves us goodbye.

'Pff, hospitals...' Niall says quietly, hobbling in.

'I'll just take you over to the desk here,' Agnes says, 'and then I'll have to love you and leave you.'

Niall doesn't crack a joke this time though. He braces himself against the reception desk and says a quiet thanks to Agnes as she leaves.

'Can I get your name please?' asks the receptionist.

Niall grimaces. 'Surprised you lot dinnae recognise me yet. Niall Robertson.'

The receptionist taps away at the computer and soon a nurse arrives with a wheelchair. Niall sits down, grimacing, and is wheeled through the doors into A&E, leg outstretched, head hung. I shout 'See you later' but he doesn't look back.

'And your name?' asks the receptionist.

'Ben Hamilton,' I say.

'We'll get you seen as soon as possible. You can take a seat for a minute if you'd like.'

I sit down on a hard plastic seat. My hand seems worse now that John's confirmed there are probably broken bones. I lift it level with my face and turn it under the fluorescent lights. The fresh blood shines in contrast to the dull burgundy crust around my fingers, and my knuckles look dark and swollen.

A nurse walks through the doors Niall was led through and stops by the reception. She looks at the clipboard in her hand, clears her throat and calls out my name.

'Well, Mr Hamilton, I'm afraid it's not great news,' says the doctor.

He tilts his PC monitor towards me to show two scans of my hand, side by side. My head got the all clear, but my hand, as they said, 'looked a mess' and they weren't wrong. Among the dark, shadowy flesh on the screen were startlingly bright bones, snapped and buckled.

'It could have been worse, I suppose. You've only actually broken a couple of bones here – the rest are just bruised.' He points at my pinkie and ring fingers, and the bones leading from them, through my hand and to my wrist. 'Fractures of the fourth and fifth metacarpal, to be technical. You're looking at around six to eight weeks recovery time.'

I lean forward, squinting at the screen. The brightness is making my eyes hurt and the consultant had warned me about other concussion side-effects. They'd also said my teeth, obviously, needed to be fixed by a dentist.

'Right,' I say. 'I see.'

The bones are broken, alright. Jagged and separate, they look more like shards of glass rather than bones split in half.

'There is also a little complication,' the doctor continues. 'This isn't your usual boxer's fracture – the bones aren't aligned anymore – and so to leave them as they are will take longer to heal, and might cause you some minor problems down the line.'

I look at him scratching at his trim beard and think about Pete – the way he always rubbed his stubble. I think about Pete and 'minor problems down the line' takes a deeper meaning. I think about his vow for revenge, like this is a game.

'Mr Hamilton?' the doctor says. 'I was saying we'll need to reposition the broken bones.'

I swallow. 'How?'

He smiles a well-rehearsed 'bad news' consolatory

smile and looks briefly at the notes on his clipboard. 'I'll need to pop them back into place. There's a nurse on her way to administer a local anaesthetic and then we can get started. Okay?'

He turns to leave before I can agree.

I sit there for a while, wondering how Niall's getting on; wondering if his leg is broken; if he's getting bones snapped back into place right this moment. As I imagine a doctor pressing down on his leg until the bones pop, a nurse walks into the room.

'Hiya, I'm here to do your anaesthetic,' she says, all sunshine and cheer.

'Thanks,' I mutter, as she takes my hand in hers and examines it.

Her skin feels rough and hard, not like the soft, smooth skin I was expecting. Then again, there are a lot of things that haven't been what I've expected recently – this is nothing in comparison.

She takes out a needle and I instinctively look away, back to the doctor's PC screen, where my bones shine like shattered porcelain. A sharp pain shoots through my palm then dulls back to gentle throbbing as the nurse pushes the needle further into my flesh, towards the bone. When it's deep enough I feel a cold sensation flood through the inside of my hand as she pushes the anaesthetic in. She pulls the needle out slowly, turns my hand, and does it again.

And again.

And again.

'Now, wait a few minutes and you should feel pins and needles, and then completely numb.'

I sit there and she stands in silence as the minutes pass and the tingling grows through my fingers and up to my wrist. I try and fail to wiggle my fingers which now feel like fat sausages. The doctor comes back and asks how we're getting on.

'Brilliant,' he says, examining my hand again. 'I'll press gently and you can tell me if you feel anything.'

He squeezes the tips of my fingers but I don't feel it. He squeezes my knuckles but again, nothing. Then, he gently squeezes my palm and I don't feel it. The pressure increases until I can see the muscles in his forearms tensing from the pressure. He's murmuring through gritted teeth 'Nearly ... nearly ... nearly ...' and then a loud snap like a firecracker fills the room.

'Brilliant,' he says again, before starting on the next bone. It yields quicker than the previous one and he stands back, proud of his handiwork.

'Right then, Mr Hamilton, we'll get you in plaster and then send you off for a final scan, okay?'

But again, before I can answer, he leaves. The nurse waits a moment and then follows, explaining over her shoulder that she'll be back to do the cast.

I think about what's happening to Niall right now. And then Pete and Jake. Wondering if they're in a hospital somewhere or recovering at home. I imagine them in a week's time, training in their back gardens: martial arts, deadly weaponry, explosive devices. *Gonna Fly Now* in the background, I see them jogging up the steps of Falkirk Sheriff Court, throwing practice punches at the top. I think about the final showdown between Eddie and his boys vs Pete and Jake. I don't think it will end well for Pete and Jake, and I can't tell if I care.

The nurse walks back in, carrying a bucket and supplies. At first I think she's here to clean up but I soon realise this is the kit for my cast. She smiles again and I still don't feel cheered or warmed by it. Just tired. She soaks a white bandage and then starts to wrap the wet fabric around my hand. I soon feel it warming up and I begin to worry it'll burn my skin, but right as I'm about to say something I feel it cool down before she applies another layer.

'How's that feeling?' she asks.

'Eh, alright, I suppose,' I say. The bandage is tight and I'm not sure if it's just-tight-enough-to-hold-my-bones-in-place or too tight. I watch my fingertips, waiting for any telltale purple tinge.

The nurse finishes with my plaster and cleans up the water that's dripping down my wrist and onto my jeans. 'That should do you then. Best of luck.'

I remember Niall's earlier comment when I joked about him getting a cast – *Aye, I'm renowned fur ma gid fortune.* The irony burns.

'I should also say,' she continues, her smile fading, 'given how you and your friend arrived here ... eh ... the police want to have a word when you're all done.'

'Great,' I say.

The nurse then asks me to follow her and I pick up my jacket with my good hand. We continue down a small corridor to another waiting area, where I sit with an x-ray card slotted between the fingers poking out from my cast. The plaster has cooled and feels solid. For a moment I consider joining Pete and Jake, using my new rock-fist as a weapon against Eddie and his boys. My mind flits back to when I was little, playing with my Street Sharks toys in school. I remember using one, Slammu, who had metal fists, to try and crush small stones in the playground.

I'm imagining crushing the bones of my enemies, a beast amongst men in that flat, darting shark-like from room to room, wreaking my revenge, venting every stress and strain I've built up since graduation, when the door to the x-ray room opens and another nurse calls my name.

'Quite a cast you've got there,' he says, closing the door behind me. 'Interesting story?'

I wonder if this is how the police will start their questioning. Innocent yet prying, while knowing full well that this is an injury born from violence. A dress rehearsal, I'm tempted to test this conversation. I don't exactly know why but I'm unsure about telling the truth. To the police or anyone who wasn't there.

I consider explaining the situation fully: telling him how I graduated with a good degree from a reputable university but still couldn't find a graduate job; how I signed on for a bit but the experience was so demeaning I cracked and started to look for any job going; how I landed a job at Asda and figured it was better than bi-weekly visits to Bathgate Jobcentre; how I tried to make new friends at work but only ended up with one mate, a pair of boys who thought I was a snob and a new gang of enemies; how I not only let a girl walk me directly into an ambush, but also fell right into that 'if she pays me attention she must desperately want me' trap; how I had my hand broken because my mate mouthed off to some guy before I even knew him; how that same mate was somewhere else in this hospital right now, potentially dealing with a broken leg and testicular cancer; how all in all, my life thus far had shaped up to be one colossal debt-inducing waste of time.

I consider running the guy through everything.

I seriously consider it.

Then, after a pause, I say 'Not really ... tripped on a kerb,' and he shrugs.

19

'Awright soldier, state ae you.' Niall shakes his head, tutting.

'Not much better yourself,' I say, nodding to his wheelchair.

'This wee hing? Ma new wheels – better than any wee Corsa fur cuttin' aboot in, Ah tell ye.'

'Looks sharp, Niall.'

He smiles briefly and then looks down to his hands, grasped tightly on the metal wheel-handle. 'How's yer paw?' he asks.

'Broken in two places,' I say. 'Badly, apparently.'

'Bet you said it didnae hurt,' Niall laughs.

'Course ... how's your leg?'

'Aw it's fine, man. The wheels are jist fur show.'

'Really, Niall,' I say. 'How is it?'

'I'm jist back fae a scan there. Won't ken 'til the doc's had a wee look at the results. He seemed happy enough, mind. Said he wis 'optimistic'. Story ae ma life, eh? First the jewels an' now ma leg? Fallin' tae bits, man.'

I don't laugh. 'Listen, Niall, I came to, eh, warn you.'

'Warn me?'

'Yeah – I just had the police round, asking all these questions.'

'Police, eh? Thought you were gonnae say Eddie an' his boys hud come back tae finish the job! Wit kindae questions?'

I sit down on a nearby chair so we're about level. He's leaning as far forward as he can with his leg stretched out, and his face is grey – fixed in concentration. It's like he's two different people: the light-hearted, joking Niall with a smile the size of the Forth Rail Bridge; or the older, more serious Niall with a heart that's heavy and a brain full of bad news. He flicks between the two so fluidly it's hard to keep up sometimes.

I lean forward too, so we're closer, like gangsters over poker, and begin.

'Mr Hamilton?' he said, dragging a seat to the middle of the room.

I nodded, taking in his hi-vis jacket and bleeping walkie-talkie. Behind him, a second officer walked in with an 'I'm so tough I walk like John Wayne' swagger. I felt conscious of my height and distinct lack of stomach.

'We're here to ask you a few questions about yourself and your friend Niall, okay?'

'Sure,' I said, 'fire on.'

They exchanged looks and the second, swaggering one – who was still standing – took out a notepad.

'Can we just establish your full name, first of all?'

'Ben Hamilton. No middle names.'

He nodded and his colleague noted this down.

'And your relationship to Mr ... Robertson?'

'Niall,' I said, 'He's a workmate.'

'Okay,' he said, nodding as though I'd answered a question much more profound. 'Now,' he continued, 'I'd like to ask you about what happened last night. We've had reports of a disturbance near Main Street in Linlithgow Bridge – a noise complaint from a resident of the local flats – and we think there might be a connection here.'

'A connection?' I asked.

'Between a noise complaint – specifically 'yelling, swearing and glass breaking' – and two young lads turning up to hospital with broken bones and what look–' he nodded to my bandaged head, '–like glass-wounds.'

I looked up at the other – glaring – officer. His pen was poised, ready to write down my response and I tried to think things through quickly.

What would Niall do? What-would-Niall-do? WhatwouldNialldo?

It felt strange thinking this, considering – to take Pete's side for a second – it *was* all technically Niall's fault. Of course I understood why Niall was acting out, and I can't say I wouldn't, but all the same, if he hadn't squared up that night in the pub ... I licked my tongue over the jagged edges of my teeth – or what's left of them.

'So, Mr Hamilton, could you please explain to us exactly what happened last night in the Main Street area of Linlithgow Bridge?'

I looked at the police officer sitting down. He was

chewing gum like a car crusher chews Vauxhalls and I swallowed a big, cartoon-style lump in my throat.

'Uhm, well, right, y'see...' A strong beginning, I thought to myself. All good lies begin this way. 'Me and Niall were walking to the off-licence there to pick up some booze.'

'Any particular reason?' the pen-toting officer asked.

'A commiseration party, I suppose. Niall got fired from Asda, y'see, so I said we should go have a couple of drinks – cheer him up, that sort of thing.'

'Why didn't you just go to a pub? You're both over 18, I presume.'

'Yeah, we are, but we fancied a quiet drink. Ironically.'

'So,' the officer sitting down said, 'you were walking about Linlithgow Bridge – then what happened?'

My mind was whirring. I had so many thoughts all blurring together I may as well have none for all the good they'd do. I tried to breathe slowly and think this through.

Both officers were looking at me expectantly.

'I don't know, to be honest.'

Was this a crime?

'We were walking one minute–'

Lying to the police must be a crime.

'–and the next minute we got jumped.'

Perjury, isn't it? Is that what this was?

'I got hit on the head with something and that's about all I can remember, until this morning.'

'So you don't remember any details at all? Who attacked you? What they looked like?'

The officer standing up was scribbling quickly. The sound of his pen seemed inordinately loud and scratched deep inside my head. I pressed my good hand to my forehead.

'Sorry, no. I wish I could help you, really, but all I remember is walking, getting hit, and then waking up.'

'Right then, Mr Hamilton, I suppose that'll do for now. We'll be in touch if we have any further questions, and if you do remember anything–' he stressed the word and I worried they knew there was more to this, '–don't forget to let us know.'

He stood up, shoulders back, as the other officer tucked away his notepad.

'I guess I shouldn't leave the country, eh?' I said, laughing weakly.

Straight faces looked back. 'We'll be paying a visit to your friend when he's ready. Maybe he'll be able to remember a bit more than you.'

'Yeah, hope so,' I said as they turned to leave.

Niall leans back, thoughtful – all he's missing is a beard to stroke.

'So ye lied?' he says.

'Well, I didn't *lie* ... I mean, I did get hit, and I don't remember a lot. I just took the events and placed them elsewhere.'

'Wi' different people. Ye didnae mention Jake an' Pete, or Hannah, Chloe. Eddie an' his boys.'

He seems angry, like I've made things worse, and my stomach clenches.

189

'Sorry, Niall ... Have I fucked up?' I ask.

He purses his lips, eyes travelling left to right. After a moment, he leans forward again. 'Naw. You've jist gone an' made it a thoosan' times easier tae git over.'

I look at him, feeling the weight lift from my shoulders and the bile vanish from my stomach.

'Now aw I need tae dae is tell the same story an' the polis will drop it – cannae investigate a random attack wi' nae clues, can they?'

'I figured you'd rather just forget about all of this, at least. Move on, y'know?'

'Aye, aye, exactly. Ye did the right hing, Ben. Sooner I can forget aw aboot Eddie, Chloe, Hannah, Jake, Pete, the sooner I can git on wi' ma life, ken?'

He smiles. His whole self seems lifted somehow. I wouldn't be surprised if he tried to walk.

'Ken, fur a posh lad wi' a degree, you've git some amount ae street-smarts aboot ye, Ben.' Niall winks.

'I like to think I've learned a thing or two from working at Asda,' I say.

'Aye, stock rotation, display assembly, lyin' tae the polis – aw in a day's work!'

I get the same feeling Niall had before, sitting on that bench waiting for the ambulance to arrive.

'Tae put it simply, Ben, all things considered, right now I'm feelin pretty fuckin' gid.'

I wonder about the future: what we're going to do after all of this – where to go from here.

'So how long are ye aw plastered up fur?' Niall asks.

'Six to eight weeks,' I say, imagining a calendar stretch out before me.

Niall puffs his cheeks, exhaling a long, slow breath. 'Fuck,' he says, 'Wit ye gonnae dae fur six tae eight weeks?'

'No idea,' I say, laughing unconvincingly, imagining a calendar of completely empty days stretch out before me.

We sit in silence for a while but it doesn't feel awkward this time. We're well-versed in sitting quietly by now. I look at Niall's leg and notice the one outstretched fills his jeans leg much more than the other. I picture what it looks like underneath the fabric, all bruised and swollen; like my hand on a bigger scale.

'So–' Niall says, after clear consideration about what to talk about now, but he's cut off as a nurse pokes her head round the curtain.

We turn to look and I know what's coming before she opens her mouth. Niall looks from her to me and then down at his leg, sighing.

'Mr Roberston? The police are here. They'd like a word.'

'Aye, send 'em in,' he says.

The two officers I met earlier walk in and stand side-by-side, looking down on Niall.

'Mr Robertson?' one asks.

'Of leg-injury fame,' Niall says.

They stand awkwardly, with no place to sit. 'We've got a few questions to ask, if you don't mind.'

'Aye, on ye's go,' Niall says, looking back at them like a matador before two bulls.

'Eh, if you don't mind...' A nod in my direction tells me to leave and I get up from my seat.

Niall waves his hand, Jedi-like and I sit back, awed by The Force. 'He can stay. Nothin' I've got tae say is private.'

Both officers fix me with a look but I hold my ground, backed up by Darth Niall. The notepad is unveiled, pen poised, and the questions begin.

'Could you tell us, Mr Robertson, what you were doing last night?'

'I wis oot wi' Ben here.'

He gestures towards me.

'For any particular reason?'

'I jist needed a night oot, y'know?
Lost ma job the other week, if ye's didnae ken.'

'And where did you go?'

The off-licence in Linlithgow Bridge, I think.

'Picked up a few cans in this wee offie,
an then went walkin' back towards my bit.'

'I see. And so what happened after you visited the off-licence?'

'Well we quite obviously got a fuckin' hidin',
didn't we?'

'Language, please, Mr Robertson. Could you tell us the details of the attack?'

No, I think.

'Well, tae put it simply, we were jist walkin'
an' then the next hing I ken Ben here goes
doon an' I git battered.'

'How many attackers were there, Mr Robertson?
Could you describe them at all?'

'Couldnae tell ye, sorry. Mair than wan, I'd say.
Came fae behind, obviously. Ben wis oot like a light an'
before I could dae anyhin I wis on the ground an' aw.
That's when ma leg got put in.'

'Right. Do you think anyone would have any motivation to attack you, Mr Robertson?'

'Attack me, officer? Nae motivation at aw. I'm a lovely
guy, see? Friend tae everycunt.'

'Second warning, Mr Robertson. And is that so?'

Is that so? I think.

'Aye. Must ae been a random attack. Mibbe some wee
neds efter a free drink.'

'Could be, Mr Robertson, could be.'

The police officers stop asking questions.

They eye Niall.

Niall eyes them.

I eye them.

And Niall.

'Well, we'll do the best we can. Although, I'm sure
you'll understand we can't really expect much with so
little evidence. We're checking local CCTV at the moment in the hope there'll be something there.'

'Mibbe find masel' on Crimewatch, eh?'

Perjury, I think.

'If you're lucky, Mr Robertson.'

'Does it look like I'm lucky?'

'Thanks for your time, both of you. We'll be in touch, and remember to let us know if anything does come to mind.'

20

The doctor pins a scan up on the light box. There, lit up in whites, blues and blacks, are an array of images of Niall's leg from different angles.

'Wit's the verdict?' Niall says, squinting up from his wheelchair.

The doctor frowns at the scan and then looks to the folder he's holding.

'Well, it's not exactly good news, but it's not the worst news you could be getting, Mr Robertson.'

Niall glances at me and then back to the doctor. I'm still looking at the scan, noticing a distinct lack of cracked or broken bones. I think about my own scan, my shadowy hand filled with jagged edges.

'Your knee,' the doctor continues, 'took the brunt of it, and in a way that's a good thing – you're very lucky you didn't break your tibia or, worse, femur.'

Niall looks at him.

'Shin and thigh bones, Mr Robertson. Luckily they're undamaged, just a little bruising to the muscles.'

Niall sighs and I look away from the scan. He looks at me again, relief in his eyes.

'So I huvnae broken ma leg?' he asks.

'No,' says the doctor. 'What you have done, however, is damaged the ligaments holding your knee together. You see, the knee is held in place by a series of ligaments all working together.'

He points his pen at the scan, indicating grey shapes among other grey shapes.

'I won't go into too much detail but basically, on either side of the knee,' he indicates the left and then right of Niall's scan, 'there are ligaments holding everything in place – the medial collateral ligament on the inside and the lateral collateral ligament on the outside.'

'Right,' Niall nods, glancing down at his knee as though amazed so much could be going on in a joint that only goes back and forth.

'You have damaged your lateral – the outside – collateral ligament, which means your knee is unstable. This is why you were able to hobble slightly, rather than having to be stretchered in earlier. There are three grades we use to measure the damage done to these ligaments: One being the lowest and three being the highest. With a Grade One tear it is a minor tear, Grade Two is more serious and Grade Three is a complete tear of the ligament.'

My mind conjures up the memory of my first day in university halls, unpacking with The Smiths playing in the background, putting up posters of Frightened Rabbit, The Fratellis and Glasvegas. A big wad of Blu-Tack in my palm, I pulled a long thick strand out. It stretched and tensed, turning white at a point in the middle before snapping with a dull crack.

'You have sustained a Grade Two tear, Mr Robertson, meaning you will have quite a recovery ahead of you.'

'How long am I looking at, doc?' says Niall, every bit the criminal sentenced for his crime.

'Hard to say, because of the nature of the tear, but you're looking at around twelve weeks potentially, with some physiotherapy after.'

'Twelve weeks...' Niall puffs, sentenced, taken down.

'Although you might be pleased to hear that you won't be needing a wheelchair.'

'I dinnae git the chair?' he says.

'You won't need one, no. Sorry, is that a disappointment?' says the doctor, perplexed.

'Wheelin' aboot would huv been a wee silver lining, aye,' Niall says, rubbing his hands on the metal wheel-handles.

'So what happens now?' I ask.

The doctor turns to me as though he's just noticed I'm here.

'He'll be given a brace or sports bandage, some crutches, and we'll arrange for him to see a physiotherapist in a little while to work out a recovery programme.'

'Christ, 'recovery programme' makes it aw sound serious, doesn't it?' Niall says, looking back from his prized wheels.

'It'll most likely be a few sessions with the physio, one-on-one, and then series of exercises to do at home and a gym routine.'

'Pfft,' Niall exhales, 'does it look like I need tae go tae the gym?'

The doctor looks at Niall, who winks, and then at me. I shrug and laugh. The doctor clears his throat. 'I've arranged for a nurse to come and fit you with a knee brace, so you should be seeing them shortly,' he says, looking back at his folder.

'Seems like nurses here do aw the real work, eh doc?' Niall says, grinning.

The doctor raises his eyebrows and leaves without saying anything.

'You've perked up,' I say, as Niall gently rolls his chair forwards and back.

'Aye, figured there's nae point wallowin', ken? Like the doc said, it could huv been worse – a worse tear, or a fuckin' broken leg – an' at least I got a shot in this mad wee chair fur a bit.'

'And an ambulance ride,' I point out.

'Oh aye,' Niall says, nodding, 'that an' aw.'

'Niall Robertson?' A voice from outside calls.

'Aye, in here,' Niall shouts.

A nurse walks in with a large blue brace in one hand and a folder in the other.

'Hiya,' she says, 'One leg brace for Mister Niall Robertson?'

'Aye, this leg here–' Niall says, nodding to his outstretched limb.

'Could have guessed,' she laughs.

'Aye, you nurses are a sharp bunch, eh? I wis jist

sayin' tae the doc, it seems like it's the nurses who dae aw the proper work in here. The doctors seem tae swan aboot tellin' everywan wits wrang wi' em, leavin' the nurses tae fix the problem.'

She laughs. 'You don't know the half of it, son. But it's nice to have someone notice the work we do.'

'Put it this way,' Niall says. 'If you didnae dae yer job right, I wouldnae exactly be leavin' here easily, would I?'

'Very true,' she says, wrapping the brace around Niall's bare leg.

His jeans are rolled up to his thigh and when she's finished with the brace she helps him roll them back down. I had thought earlier that his jeans looked fuller around his knee, but now they're stretched as far as possible around his braced joint.

'Right, that's you then.'

'Cheers. Appreciate it,' Niall says.

The nurse smiles and turns to leave, smiling at me as she goes. I'm amazed at how many of them seem happy despite their surroundings. If I worked in a hospital, surrounded by sick people, dealing with patients who are injured, ill or dying, I can't imagine I'd be full of sunshine and bunnies. But then I figure, to them it's a job – their work. You clock in, clock out the same as anyone else; deal with a list of chores the same as anyone else; put up with the public being rude to you the same as anyone else. To put it bluntly, you deal with it. I start to wonder how well I've been dealing with my job, my work, as Niall rubs his hand over his braced knee.

'Feels weird,' he says. 'Constricting.'

'I guess that's good though,' I say.

'Aye, definitely. Dinnae want ma knee ... y'know ... fallin' aff.'

I laugh as the doctor returns.

'Awright, doc?' Niall says, and I gather from the doctor's shiver that he's growing tired of Niall's 'doc' treatment.

'You're all braced up then, Mr Robertson?' he says.

'I am, aye,' Niall replies.

'Well, then you're all set. I've made you an appointment with the physiotherapist here, and all the details are on this.' He hands Niall a small square card and looks back at his folder. I figure this is probably a reflex for him now, having done it so often, every day, for so long.

'There's a set of crutches here for you as well. So unless you have any questions or anything, you're free to go.'

Niall peers past him at the standard grey NHS crutches and shakes his head. 'Naw, that's me, doc. Glad tae be on ma way. Ta fur yer help, mind,' he says.

I'm beginning to wonder if Niall's acting this way to wind the doctor up; to get some sort of fun out of his hospital visit. Another hospital visit.

Niall tries to stand and I help him up. He leans on me heavily as the doctor passes us the crutches, and Niall sinks into them easily. He crutch-walks out, past the doctor, and away down the corridor. I say thanks to the doctor and a quick 'Eh, sorry about ... y'know ... him', and follow.

'Aww Ben, I tell ye, I am fuckin' sick of hospitals. Fuckin' sick ae them.'

'I can understand why, Niall,' I say, shivering in the cold. We rang a taxi twenty minutes ago but it still hasn't arrived.

'It's like I fuckin' live in 'em now. Might as well start payin' rent on a wee bed ae ma ain – prob'ly cheaper than a flat.'

'And dirtier,' I say.

He laughs, but like me, it's obvious the cold is getting to him.

'Some fucking weather we get here, isn't it?' I say, my teeth starting to chatter.

'Salt in the wound, Ben. There's that nurse tellin' ye no' tae git that cast wet an' wit happens when ye leave the ward?' He nods his head to the grey clouds above us. A light shower is starting and I watch the rain distort existing puddles in the car park. My cast is stuck inside my jacket sleeve, too big to push through, but at least this keeps it dry.

'You sure this isn't gonna cost us, like, a hundred quid?' I ask.

'Aye, taxi fae here tae Lithgae should be aboot twenty, I reckon.'

'I once paid forty for a cab in Glasgow, by accident,' I say, my mind racing back to the next morning, checking my wallet and bank slips.

'How the fuck did that happen?' Niall asks, shaking his head, his eyes still fixed on the road in front of us.

'I meant to give the guy a twenty but must have given him two together by accident. Didn't notice 'til I was back in my flat.' I feel my cheeks flush red.

'Well, aren't you a right Robin Hood? Takin' a student loan fae the rich tax-payer an' givin' it tae the poor taxi driver. I'm lookin' pretty skint these days...' Niall laughs, winking at me, his palm outstretched like a beggar crying 'alms' in the street.

'Alright, alright, as if it wasn't a painful memory enough. At least you've got your wallet, remember? I'm the one needing some fucking charity right now.'

'Eh, I hink I'm needin' aw the charity I can git, Ben. Look at the fuckin' state ae me. Wan leg all battered up, an' some dodgy fuckin' baws that might be the fuckin' end ae me.'

'Don't say that – you said yourself there's, what, a 90, 95% chance of beating it? IF it even is cancer.'

'Aye, they say that, Ben, but ye dinnae git wit it feels like, knowin' there's sumhin in your body no' workin' properly, knowin' there's sumhin doon there that could *potentially* spread aw through me ... At least I ken ma knee will git better, y'know? I ken it willnae git worse, or spread. But jist hinkin' aboot cancer getting mair ae a haud on me...' He shudders. 'There's no guarantee about beatin' cancer, despite any wee figures an' odds they give ye. It aw jist depends on chance. An anyway, it's no' even jist that wit scares me.'

Niall shivers again, harder. I hear the crutches clatter like a drum roll against the wall he's leaning against.

'What d'you mean?' I ask.

'Huv you no' seen people wi' cancer? People on chemo? Nae hair, skinny, gaunt, weak, y'know? Man, that terrifies me.'

'You might not even need chemo, though, remember?'

'Aye, but you ken wit I will need, if the doc says it's cancer. Ask yersel', can you imagine only huvin' wan baw?'

The wind blows across the car park: a howling, roaring gust, bringing dust and rain and crisp packets.

'There's the taxi,' I say, shuddering.

A grey car pulls up and the driver winds the window down.

'Car for Hamilton?' he shouts, his words almost swallowed up by the wind.

I nod and Niall opens the back door. He lowers himself in gently, keeping his leg outstretched as he shuffles across the back seat. I hand his crutches in after him and shut the door. The heating is on full blast in the front and I feel my feet tingle as they start to warm.

'Fuck's sake,' the driver says, pulling out of the car park, 'state of you two. What happened?'

'Asked too many stupid questions in a taxi,' Niall says, looking out of the window as bus stops slip by.

The driver adjusts the sat-nav and I see him rolling his eyes as the machine beeps and the screen changes to show a small map of the back roads to Linlithgow, past the farms and over the hills. A pastoral taxi journey made edgy by Niall's mood swings. I look out of the window and catch my reflection instead. I only look for a moment, but my eyes are drawn to my sleeve, thick and full with my cast, before I change my focus and look out of the windscreen to see the roads, now dark and slick with rain, roll underneath us as we drive.

21

'Niall,' I say, leaning round to face the back seat. He's still looking out of the window, eyes darting as he watches the fences and farm buildings pass.

'Niall,' I say again. His eyes flick to me and then away out of the window again.

'Long John fucking Silver,' I say, and his eyebrows wrinkle.

'Wit?' he says.

'Sorry, cheap shot, I know.'

He smiles but tries to straighten his face so I don't notice.

'I know I've mentioned it already but I can't stop thinking about it – d'you think Jake and Pete really *are* going to carry on with all this gang-war shit?'

He sighs and glances out of the window again. A herd of cows flit past, enduring the rain, their mouths full of wet grass.

'I mean, I know you said you didn't really care, but ... y'know ... I do,' I continue.

'Honestly? Aye, they very well might. Pete disnae strike me as the kindae guy tae jist take shit an' smile, ken? An' Jake's too busy tryin' tae fit his heid up Pete's arse tae notice wit's goin on.'

I imagine them, stalking round Falkirk, hand-tools in their coat pockets, waiting for Eddie's boys to finish work. Then, one by one, hammering or chiselling or Stanley-knifing their revenge across Central Scotland. It'd be like *The Crow* with more rain.

'I'm kindae hopin' they'll leave it, tae be honest. Last hing I want is another batterin' fae they boys 'cause they hink I wis in on it.'

'I'd not thought of that,' I say, now solely thinking of that.

I imagine Eddie and his boys, stalking round Linlithgow, hand-tools in their coat pockets, waiting for Niall outside his house.

'Fuck...' he sighs, eyes fixed out of the window again. 'I jist want oot ae this situation, y'know? I wish there wis an eject button tae blast me intae the sky. I'd land in fuckin' ... Tennessee or somewhere. Kindae place none ae this gang shit happens.'

'Or a rewind button,' I say. 'Take me back to living in a flat in Glasgow: classes all day, reading books all night.'

'Sounds like you were a shite student, Ben. Thought you were meant tae be aw perties an' drinkin' an' skippin' lectures.'

'Nah, I was never into all that. Figured if I was lucky enough to go to uni I should make the most of it.'

'Aye, right enough. See if I couldae gone tae uni, I

would ae DEVOURED they books, man. I'd want tae be the smartest fucker in the class,' Niall says, determined, as though *Ulysses* is sitting in front of him with a side of salad.

'Not that it really did me much good in the end, eh?' I say.

'No' yet,' Niall replies. 'But you dinnae ken wit's aroon the corner – like wit ye telt me about seein' a shitey situation wi' Asda as a possibility tae dae sumhin else; this shitey situation might be the start ae a change fur you, ken?'

I'm not sure if it's what Niall's saying or the heating finally managing to reach my bones and returning me to 37 degrees, but I feel so warmed by this I temporarily forget all about my hand, Niall's leg, Niall's diagnosis, the pissing rain, everything. For a moment.

I smile and he's nodding his head, deep in thought.

'So what now?' I ask, bringing Niall's attention back to the present.

'Now I am goin hame fur a fuckin' Pot Noodle, a big glass ae juice an' a huge fuckin' sleep,' Niall laughs.

'No, not like that,' I say. 'I mean, what do we do now? That pact to get out of here...'

'Aw, I see. Well, I've been hinking. An' dinnae laugh when I tell ye 'cause I could still fuckin' pound ye even wi' a knackered knee ... but ... an' it's jist a wee idea, still mullin' it over, ken? But ... I wis hinkin ae goin tae college.'

He says this like he's just announced he's going to walk to California.

'What d'you want to study?' I ask, serious-face on.

Niall is taken aback, as though he was expecting me to laugh his plan off. 'Eh, well, mind when we were talkin' the other day aboot wit we wanted tae be when we were wee? An' I said I used tae want tae be in The Corries?'

'Yeah, I remember.'

'Well I wis kindae hinkin aboot mibbe gettin back intae playin' guitar properly, an' goin' tae college tae study some kindae music course. Mibbe. Wit d'ye hink?'

I think about it for a moment and I can see Niall tense, still waiting for me to shoot down his plans and tell him he's aiming too high.

'Go for it,' I say.

'Wit?'

'Go for it. Why not? You can play an instrument and you've always wanted to do something musical.'

'Ye hink I should dae it?' he asks, amazed.

'Yeah, totally.'

He's grinning now, that same grin I saw in the hospital, but without the mischievous edge.

'"Cause ma mum did a course at Forth Valley a couple ae year ago – said it wis really gid,' he continues, his words higher and faster now.

'It's pretty local too,' I point out.

'Aye, exactly. I wouldnae need that much money fur it, y'know? If I stayed at hame, mibbe took a wee loan affae ma mum tae cover the fees. Then I could move away once I finished.'

'Sounds like a plan,' I say, as the taxi driver starts whistling. A cheery tune, it sounds thoroughly Scottish in a way I'm surprised to find comforting. I wait for Niall to tell him to stop, or to belt him with a crutch, but he doesn't.

'You like The Corries?' Niall asks, and the driver turns his head.

'Eh?'

'*Scotland Will Flourish*, no?' Niall says, nodding approvingly.

'Is it?' says the driver, slowing as we drive past a sign saying Welcome to the Royal Burgh of Linlithgow. 'I didn't know – heard it on the radio the other day and I can't get it out of my head.'

'Aye, it's The Corries, right enough,' Niall says, in his element. He sings to himself and I try leaning closer to hear better. Lyrics about working hard for a better life. Forgiveness. Kinship. Nationhood.

The taxi driver has lost interest, studying the sat-nav for the best route to Niall's house, but I'm enthralled listening to Niall's whispered lyrics. I feel something now, like the warmth I was feeling earlier, but stronger: something in my chest, my stomach. A tingling sensation floods to my broken hand and I wiggle my fingertips to help improve the blood flow. The tingling doesn't stop though. Instead, it washes back to my very core and I begin to think it's more than constricted nerves. Maybe, and the thought becomes more convincing the more Niall recites, it's hope. The strong tingling of hope rising in my stomach, spreading up past my lungs, scratching the back of my throat, making me salivate until it comes, wet and stinging, into my mouth. The acrid, bitter taste of hope.

Or vomit. I clamp my lips shut and try to will myself to avoid a £40 excess charge. Swallowing, I suppress the hope deep back into my body and try to pretend everything is normal.

'Is this us then, lads?' the taxi driver says, cutting Niall's singing off.

I see Niall's house one door down.

'Yeah,' I say, pleased I wasn't sick but sad not to hear those lyrics anymore.

I get out of the taxi and walk round to open Niall's door, but he's beaten me to it.

'No' a total waste ae space,' he says, laughing as he swings his damaged leg out onto the street.

He passes me the crutches and I help him heave his weight from the car to the sticks. He seems unsteady for a moment but he soon finds his gait.

'How much d'we owe you?' I ask the driver, my head level with his unwound window.

'Eighteen,' he says, glancing at a chart he pulled down from his sun visor.

'Call it twenty,' Niall says, handing me a note.

The driver nods as I pass it to him and he pulls away, his tyres spraying a fine cloud of water from the puddles.

'You alright getting in?' I ask.

Niall glances round at his front door.

'Aye, be fine. Got tae git used tae daein' this maself.'

'Yeah,' I say.

'So, eh, thanks, Ben.'

'You paid for the taxi – thank you.'

'Hope yer hand gets better soon,' Niall says, nodding at my sleeve.

'Same for your leg. Let me know how everything goes, yeah?'

Niall nods, says 'Aye' and turns away. He swings his leg forward and bit by bit edges up towards his front door.

I watch him until he's inside and then leave. I reach for my phone, my good hand patting my pocket for a moment before I remember I don't have it anymore. I walk, no phone, no music to distract me. Just the thoughts of the past however-many hours and the memory of that tingling feeling I had for a brief, queasy moment as Niall whispered words sung about a better Scotland.

I flick through my old Facebook messages, tracing the ebb and flow of friendships through my years at university; watching people fall in and out of my life; remembering old jokes I'd long forgotten about; remembering people I'd tried not to think about as well.

Email:.........................
Password: ....

Sender: Ashley Webb

Hey hey Benny, how're you? Not seen you since graduation – 2 months is too long! What have you been up to? How's life etc? Just wanted to touch base, see how my favourite future-teacher is doing. We should go for a drink some time.

A x

To: Ashley Webb

Hi Ashley,

Yeah, long time. I'm good, thanks. How about you?

It's been crazy recently. I've been applying for so many jobs I'm losing track. Fingers crossed one of them will come through though. How's your placement going? Must be exciting being a hot-shot lawyer!

Definitely. Where and when?

Ben.x

Sender: Ashley Webb

I'm great. Placement is amazing. Loads of great experience but it's SO hectic. I spend most of my time off sleeping! I'll keep my fingers crossed for you – what sort of stuff are you applying for? How about 8 next Saturday, at The Cellars?

A x

To: Ashley Webb

I can imagine. You're well suited to it though – I don't think I've ever won an argument with you...

I'm looking at a mixture of stuff really.

Publishing jobs, editing, copywriting – general English grad jobs, really. I'm trying to get some teaching experience too, so I'm waiting to see if any schools might let me come sit in with a class or something. Figured that'd help with a postgrad application.

That sounds great. See you there.

Have you seen much of anyone else recently?

Ben.x

Sender: Ashley Webb

Well good luck! Not really, to be honest. I met Dean in Sainsburys a couple of weeks back – he'd just started his probation year in a primary school. Not seen Amy since graduation. She's probably a millionaire by now! What about yourself?

A x

To: Ashley Webb

Nah, not seen anyone, to be honest. Seems like we all went our separate ways after we got our diplomas. Bit of a shame but I guess that's how life goes. Pursue your dreams and all that.

Ben.x

Log Out

With a flash of decisiveness, I start to write. My eyes fix on the screen, glancing down every now and again to correct my one-handed typing. A short message, casual, friendly. Hiding my genuine concern.

Alright Niall? Just wondering how you're doing. Let's get together for a drink sometime – be good to talk things through away from hospitals and high street pubs. Let me know.

I hit the return key and watch the message display.
Sent.

I flex my fingers slowly, both hands. My bad hand feels still and confined but I'm getting used to the cast. It's the least of my worries, at any rate. Earlier, coming home to a blissfully empty house, I'd fallen asleep face-down on my bed. I must have only been out for about five minutes when I woke with a start. Dreams about Chloe's foot hammering down on my fragile fingers. Later on I woke to the sound of someone moving around the house. Panicked, I hid, childlike, under the covers until Eddie and his boys (or, as it turned out, my dad home from work) went away. I'd stopped seeing a drowned woman everywhere I looked – was a new paranoia starting? Would I turn into one of those people who could never leave their house?

So this was my shot – my cry for help to someone who might be able to understand. Pete and Jake were obviously in a totally different frame of mind (and probably wouldn't talk to me anyway), and my parents were now too busy telling the neighbours that hoodlums – yes, real, live, cigarette-smoking, hoodie-wearing ruffians – roamed the streets of their quiet little town, assaulting anyone who wasn't on crack cocaine or carrying a meat cleaver to protect themselves.

I wait the rest of the night for a reply, figuring someone with a torn ligament wouldn't be doing much else other than sitting in bed killing time. No reply comes. I wait the next day, too, 'liking' groups and old photos so that my profile will display recent activity – so that my profile will scream LOOK, I'M ONLINE, HERE, NOT GOING ANYWHERE, WAITING FOR YOU. Still no reply comes. And it is then, on the second day with no response, that I find myself remembering that meeting with Ashley, when we went out for a drink, shortly before I moved away from Glasgow.

We had met with smiles and hugs and 'How are you?'s and 'Not bad, thanks's and quickly gotten round to drinking. One of my closest friends at uni, Ashley had always been a source of friendly encouragement, infallible reasoning and, of course, nightly winnings from pub quiz machines. But midway through the night out I noticed something had changed. We were no longer swapping stories about mutual friends or lecturers or the landlord. We were no longer laughing so hard our ribs hurt. We were no longer clicking like good friends do.

I had realised then, as she walked back from the toilets, that we were drinking to soothe the uneasy atmosphere between us, nodding and laughing about stories from nights we weren't at with people we didn't know. To put it plainly, we were strangers again. She had sat down and reached for her drink, smiling in a way I now saw as awkward, rather than friendly. I had sipped my pint and tried to think for something to say. Eventually, after three mouthfuls of lager, I'd coughed out the first fully-formed thing that came to mind.

'D'you not think it's weird that we're not all friends anymore?'

The uncomfortable atmosphere was out in the open then. I'd blow it up right in both of our faces, shrapnel and viscera flying everywhere.

'I guess it's like how I don't really see any of my old secondary school friends anymore,' she'd said. 'People just move on. They grow, change, whatever, and sometimes you lose friends. It's just part of life, y'know?'

'Yeah, I totally get why it happens. I just think it's a shame. You, me, Dean and Amy were like a team, all the way through uni. Four years, you know? It's just a shame that none of us really see each other anymore, that's all.'

'We'll see each other at the reunion,' Ashley said. 'You and Dean will both be headmasters, Amy will be running a multi-billion pound business empire and I'll be defending activists in the European courts. Just you wait.'

She had laughed, teetering between genuine and awkward, and I knew then that the night was over.

'And anyway,' she'd continued, 'it's the ones who cling on to old friendships – friendships that maybe should be put to bed – that you need to worry about.'

As I sit, slowly spinning on the old office chair in my old room in my parents' house, I begin to wonder about me and Niall: except this time not about our broken bones or Eddie and his boys tracking us down for round two. I begin to wonder if maybe this is our turn to move on, to drift apart, much the same as Dean, Ashley, Amy and I had done after graduation. And as I wonder, still turning, seeing my Asda uniform spin past me in a black and green pile on the radiator, it dawns on me that actually, instead of going our own separate ways, perhaps Niall – planning on going off to college, going off away from Linlithgow with its pubs and friends and rivals – is just ready to begin leaving me behind.

22

'Awright Ben?' Niall says, the phone line distant and fuzzy. My new phone hadn't recognised the number but I know his voice. 'Long time, eh?'

'Uhm, yeah, it has been. How are you?' I reply, hearing traffic now too.

'Gettin' there, aye. Walkin' by masel' again, though, which is nice. No' on they crutches anymair. Wit aboot yersel'?'

'Good to hear. I'm alright, thanks. Cast came off a while back and my teeth got fixed a couple of days after I last saw you.'

'Nice wan. Nice wan. Listen, I wis wunnerin' if ye fancied that drink?'

I hear him cough away from the phone. It's been weeks, months almost, since I sent him that message. Why now?

'Sure. A drink sounds good,' I say.

'Ye free the night?'

'Uh...' I pretend to think. 'Yeah, I am, actually.'

'See ye at the Auld Hole aroon eight?'

'The Auld Hole? Like, The Auld Hole in the Wall?' I say, surprised at his choice of pub.

wan ae you boys pulled a blade on me last week

'Aye, the very same. I'm playin' a gig.'

'A gig?' I say, conscious of how many questions I'm asking in the same stunned tone.

'See ye there.'

A beep in my ear and the phone line goes silent.

Did I hear him right? A gig? I glance at the clock – 6:45pm. Enough time to get ready, but a gig? In the Auld Hole? Maybe Niall had been up to more in the past few weeks than I was actually expecting. Course, I knew he wanted to pursue a music course; he had seemed totally serious about that when he told me, but I wasn't expecting things to happen so quickly.

I feel a glimmer of guilt for my reaction. Of course I want the best for Niall. That's why I encouraged him to enrol in college. But I also want the best for me, and it seems like so far, only one of us has had their way.

I work out a routine, chopping the clock up into neat slices in my head, leaving enough time to walk to the pub for eight on the dot. Meeting someone who's seen you with a broken hand and no teeth means you needn't bother with being fashionably late, I figure.

Shower: 10 mins. Dry and dress: 15 mins. Hair: 10 mins. Dinner (cook and eat): 25 mins.

Military style, this anxious soldier gets ready. I stand to attention in front of the mirror, ready for inspection. Jeans, shirt, faux-leather shoes on. Dusted and neat.

Hair, reasonable – needs a trim though, Private. With everything in place (except my rifle) I run down to the kitchen to start on my dinner.

'Going somewhere nice?' Mum asks, squinting out through the window. 'You might need a jacket – it looks cold outside.'

'Just the pub, and yes, Mother, of course I'll take a jacket. Dad still at work?'

'On his way back, apparently. Another late finish,' she sighs, glancing at the clock. 'You try and stay safe tonight, okay?'

After chucking a quick dinner down my throat, I close the front door behind me and start to walk down towards the canal. Mum was right – it is cold and I did need a jacket. I pull my hands from my pockets and tap out a quick message to the number I saved after Niall's call.

Be there soon. Whereabouts are you?

A few minutes later, as I pass the canal and take the alley down to the High Street, my phone beeps.

Sound. Ill be the cunt wi nae broken legs ;) Ye canny miss me.

The Auld Hole in the Wall is a pub that brings back memories of running, possibly for our lives, through Linlithgow High Street. Classic exterior design masking the place where Niall, Pete, Jake and I nearly got stabbed what seems like a lifetime ago. The interior is fairly standard. Tonight it has a young vibe. The board outside is decorated in coloured chalk, advertising 3 for 2 deals,

£1 shots and A LIVE BAND! I take a deep breath and walk in. Aftershave, perfume, vodka.

It's totally rammed and I have to squeeze through groups of drinkers to get to the bar. The barmaid comes over after serving a loud group down the other end and leans across, offering an ear weighted down with large hoops. I ask for a pint of Tennent's but she cups her ear again.

'Pint of TENNENT'S, please.' I hand over a note and she walks back to the till before returning to the taps.

She pours: the liquid swilling and frothing as it rises to the top of the glass. The foam get thicker and thicker until it spills down the side, at which point the barmaid stops the tap and hands me my drink.

'Ye here fur the band?' shouts a voice next to me.

A nudge in my ribs as I turn and I see Niall holding a pint, grinning.

'Alright stranger,' I say.

'I ken, hardly recognised ye there!'

He motions for me to follow and together we squeeze and shuffle through the mass of people until we get to a table at the back, next to a pool table currently occupied by a group of serious-looking men. It looks like there's money riding on the game and their quiet, considered vibe is clearly the reason Niall's sitting so far from the bar.

'I see the hand's daein' awright,' Niall says, nodding to my fingers, clasped tightly around the beer.

'Yeah, not bad. They said it healed well and it's probably actually stronger now because of it.'

'So ye can go an' hammer anywan ye want now?' Niall winks.

'That's exactly what the doctor said, yeah,' I laugh. 'How's your leg? Can't have been long since you got your cast off.'

'Leg's nae bad. They took the cast aff early an' put me intae this pure intense physio routine. Said I wis beastin' through ma recovery, so as of two weeks ago I am officially healed.'

The word 'healed' hangs in the air for a moment, imbued with such strong sentiment that it says so much more about Niall than his smile, or lack of crutches.

'That's amazing,' I say. 'Good news all round then.'

'That's no' even aw ae it,' Niall says, a smile playing at the edges of his mouth.

'I was meaning to say, I remembered you saying you were due the results and I kept trying to get in touch with you, but your house is ex-directory and you weren't responding on Facebook–'

'I'm fine,' Niall cuts me off, grinning so hard I'm afraid his head might split in two.

'You're fine?' I say, the smile spreading to my face as well now.

'Clean and clear as a whistle,' he says. 'Turns oot the lump wis this hing called a cyst. Totally harmless, jist a wee bag ae fluid, basically. Wit did he say? ... *Benign*, aye that's the wan. A benign cyst. Doc said guys get them aw the time. Mine looked fair dodgy at first but they tests proved it wis nuthin' tae worry aboot.'

222

'That's amazing! Wow, congratulations!' I say, raising my glass to benign testicular cysts everywhere.

Niall raises his beer too, and continues. 'He said it can be painful at times an' they could remove it if it starts tae be a problem, but fur now aw I need tae dae is keep an eye on it.'

'And that's it? No pills or surgery or anything?' I ask.

'Nuthin' at aw,' Niall beams. 'Sound as a pound, me.'

We clink glasses and drink deeply. Suddenly, with the drop of a hat – or cyst – this reunion has turned into a huge celebration.

'Well, I bet that brightened your life up,' I say, 'getting that good news.'

'Totally, man, totally,' Niall says, licking the beer froth from his top lip. 'I wis so afraid it wis gonnae be bad, y'know? An' when the doc wanted me tae come in tae the surgery I wis convinced. Convinced. But I sat doon an' the doc swung roon in his chair pure smilin', an' he slapped this wee folder doon on his desk an' I jist knew. His face said it aw.'

'Mr Robertson,' he said, 'you'll be pleased to hear it is good news. You don't have cancer.'

'Man, if I couldae framed they words it'd be up on ma livin' room wall instead ae a telly.'

He laughs and I can see it: I can actually see how alive he is as he sits there, laughing. He's probably not even laughing about what he's just said. He's just laughing.

'So what happened next?' I ask. 'You got the good news and then what?'

'Aw, man, I'll tell ye. Ken how I said I wis gonnae go tae college an' study, aye?'

I nod, drinking my pint to halfway.

'Well, I figured there's nae point in applyin' only tae find oot I'm gonnae die halfway through the course, so I put it aff 'til the doc said I wis awright. Then, that day, I phoned up Forth Valley, ken that wan in Fawkirk ma mum went tae? I phoned them an' jist burst, man. I telt them everyhin aboot ma cancer scare, puttin' aff applyin', the whole deal. An' naw, by the way, I didnae tell them aboot gettin' jumped – figured that wee chapter wisnae relevant tae ma story. But anyways, efter I'd finished talkin', the wuman on the end ae the line jist goes 'Uhm, I'll direct you to a Learning Advisor'. Turns oot I'd telt the whole story tae a receptionist!'

I splutter into my pint, wetting my nose and splashing beer across the bar mats. The pool-playing men shoot looks like I just pissed on their table, but soon return to their game.

'So what happened then?' I ask.

'I jist repeated the whole hing an' they said they could fast-track ma application 'cause I'd missed the deadline. A while later a nice wee letter pops through ma door sayin' 'Congratulations, Mr Niall Robertson, we would like to offer you a place on the HND Sound Production course'. An' here I am.'

He grins again then drains his pint.

'An' I ken, I shouldae telt ye. I'm sorry fur totally cutting ye oot like that, I am. But I jist needed a bit ae space, y'know? I needed tae sort masel' oot an' I jist didnae hink I could if I hud any sort ae reminders aboot here, aboot wit happened, ken?'

'Yet you arranged to meet me *here*, in *this* pub?' I say.

He shifts in his seat, pushes his glass towards the centre of the table.

'Two hings – first of all, couldnae help it. Ma band git booked tae play here, so I could hardly go 'Eh, sorry, guys, but I nearly got masel' killt in that pub once', could I? An' number two, it's aw water under the bridge, ken? Ye've got tae move on wi' yer life. D'ye really hink they boys who jumped us, or Pete an' Jake fur that matter, are really still gunnin' fur us?'

I consider his question but don't answer. I'm in two minds – literally fifty/fifty.

Yes, they probably are still after us.

And no, of course not. It all peaked. The pot boiled.

It's over.

I know which one I'd like to believe.

'So you've got a band now,' I say, not-at-all-subtly changing the conversation.

'Aye, I dae. Promise of the Day, we're called. First week ae class we got asked who played instruments an' it jist sort ae aw went fae there.'

'Where are they now?' I ask, looking around.

'Probably fucked off tae get sumhin tae eat, or still fannyin' aboot wi' Charlie's drums. He wis complainin' earlier 'cause some cunt bumped intae his cymbal stand an' nearly knocked it ower. Drummers, eh?'

I laugh, nodding my head with no real idea if drummers are famous for their prima donna attitudes.

'Actually,' Niall says, peering over my shoulder, 'that's them there.'

I turn and see three figures at the bar looking over at their equipment protectively.

'Obviously the guy is Charlie, on drums, an' the two lassies are Ann and Lauren, singer and bassist.'

'What sort of music do you play?' I ask, remembering Niall's childhood ambition of joining The Corries anxiously.

'Kindae pop/rock. Or rock/pop. Y'know? Bit ae Britpop, bit ae this, bit ae that. A nice mix ae stuff.'

'Sounds good,' I say.

'Actually,' Niall says, peering back over towards the bar, 'away an' git yersel' another pint, Ben, an' you'll find oot. That's us on the now.'

Ann, Charlie and Lauren make their way towards their gear and as I get up Niall dodges past me, spritely on his healed legs.

'Good luck,' I shout as he weaves past drinkers to get to his guitar.

Niall turns as he walks, grinning again, face cleaved in two with teeth and joy, and yells back.

'Like I need luck anymair!'

23

Niall slides himself to the left, shifts to the right, takes a step forward, tilts his head back, eyes shut, mouth wide. Blissful in the moment, he picks out a gentle melody on the guitar before shattering the ambience by stamping on his distortion pedal as the rest of the band join in, bass growling, drums crashing. He strums out crunchy chords as Ann starts to sing. Her voice cuts through the music, notes perfect, high and clear.

My hand clasped round another pint, I notice I'm actually holding it a bit too tight: my knuckles are pale with the stress. It's like that moment you hear about from religious people: when they're standing looking at a relic or church or something and all of their old atheist thoughts fly out of their head as a beam of light – literal or otherwise – holds them still, as they come to realise that actually, everything *does* make sense.

Niall pushes his guitar down with another chord spitting from his amp. Charlie's crashing hard on the cymbal to his right, his bass and snare drums punctuating the music like a heartbeat. Lauren slides her finger down the fretboard as the chords change and then hammers out the new note like a workie hitting home a nail. And Ann, there, holding on to the microphone stand, one hand cupped gracefully around the mic itself, eyes shut, holds on to one perfect note as the chorus ends and the band launch into the coda.

'Thanks. That was one we wrote ourselves,' Ann says, smiling, her eyes now open, scanning the crowd.

The applause dies down and there's a squeak of feedback as Niall changes the settings on his pedal.

'And that was the first time we've ever played it outside rehearsal,' Ann continues, 'So, uhm, yeah. This is our first gig, so it's really the first time we've played any ae these songs outside rehearsal.'

There's a ripple of laughter at the front, where the crowd breaks tide-like before the band. The Auld Hole doesn't have a stage, so the only thing stopping drunks from rushing the band is the knowledge that guitars hurt when they're swung, and drummers hit hard for a living.

I take a sip of my beer as Charlie counts in, the chick of his hi-hats silencing those who were still talking. The song begins, both familiar and strange at the same time and it's not until Ann sings the first line that I work out it's *A Design For Life* by the Manic Street Preachers. It seems I'm not the only one just coming to this realisation and there's a late cheer from a few groups at the back who, when I turn to look, are swaying their drinks in the air to the 6/8 beat.

It's right then – as Lauren walks slowly in little circles and Niall plucks out the broken chords, nodding his head to the beat – that I realise Niall is exactly where he should be: on stage, with a band, studying his passion at college. And it's weird thinking that this change, this milestone, came about because he had a cancer scare, got fired from his shit job, and got attacked. But now he's here, in the pub we once got chased out of, on stage, in a band, at college. Happy.

Niall swings his guitar as the chorus breaks, washing over the crowd who, with drinks in the air, all sing along in their drunken Scottish voices. It's during this perfect moment – as I'm belting the words out at the top of my lungs, and the only thing inside my head (for what feels like the first time since I moved back to Linlithgow) is the thought that **this is what life is supposed to be about** – that I glance out of the corner of my eye and see Eddie push through the crowd and approach the bar.

> *there's only wan way oot ae here an' it's that*
> *fucking door*
> *Ben, I see you've taken a wee fancy tae ma girlfriend*
> *Wan ae you boys pulled a blade on me last week*

He leans over the bar, orders his drinks and turns round to shout something across at the people he's with. Fucking Eddie.

My heart is battering the inside of my ribs harder than Charlie's beating his snare drum and my eyes flick through the crowd, scanning each face for a trace of recognition. I blink and when I look again I see them.

Mikey, Hannah, Chloe, the other guy. The whole gang, out for a quiet drink.

I look back to the band. Niall's oblivious, singing along, strumming his guitar like a rock star. Charlie's red in the face now, puffing as he pounds out beats, and Lauren's jumping on the spot, singing along as well. Ann's waving one arm above her head, directing the crowd who, like a dazed audience in front of a hypnotist, mirror her movements, singing at the top of their alcohol-fuelled voices. She smiles at Niall, then at Lauren and Charlie. This isn't only Niall's dream come true.

I imagine the smile vanishing from her face as Eddie and his gang push their way towards the band and start mercilessly pounding her guitarist until he falls amongst shattered glass, feedback squeaking, band mates screaming, until the bouncers work their way through the crowd. And I'd be standing there, knowing that as long as I stay here in Linlithgow, this would be the threat I'd have to live with.

I turn my head back, looking out for Eddie and his group of mates, but can't spot them among the crowd. Someone else has taken Eddie's place at the bar and I spin round, frantically searching for them. I feel like a small vulnerable animal out in the wild who's just heard a twig snap amongst the trees. The band start another song and I recognise it straight away. *Wonderwall* by Oasis. The classic cover. Ann sings perfectly, avoiding the oh-so-often-made mistake of adopting a Gallagher accent, but the words don't wash over me this time. God's beam of light has dimmed and I don't feel alone in a religious, beautiful way anymore. I feel vulnerable. A surfer in open water.

The music stops. It's that bit with the drum fill, and Charlie nails it. But for all his drumming skill the band may as well have played the Jaws theme as   dun-un   dun-dun   dun-dun-dun-dun-dun-dun   the shark must be getting closer and closer, smelling my fear, my movement as electrical signals in the water and then, right as the music climaxes, someone pushes past me and some of my drink spills, dribbling down my shirt. I look up and there, standing right in front of me, watching the lager soak into the fabric on my chest, is Eddie.

He looks at me, eyes sharp, and I swear I can read his thoughts as though printed on his retinas. He's trying to place me. He's sure he's seen me before, but where? Where does he know me from?

I look back at him, rabbit in the headlights of a lorry speeding towards me.

'Sorry,' he says, deadpan.

My tongue doesn't seem to work and I can't think of any words. My brain fumbles for a moment, surprised that there isn't a fist connecting with my jawbone, or shards of glass imbedded in my scalp. Again.

'No worries,' I say, and he walks off.

As he merges back into the crowd I'm left with an odd feeling. Elated, confused, headrush-y. Like a pedestrian who's narrowly dodged a speeding car. I brush myself down, checking limbs, fingers, feet. I'm fine. I'm still here, intact. The Jaws theme fades away.

I finish my pint, drinking deeply as my heart rate returns back from hummingbird to human. The beer hits my stomach and I feel it instantly. Warm, filling. I pretend it was whisky thrown back after a hard day at the office. A really hard day. A day so hard I need more.

'Yes?' says the barmaid, leaning over, again offering her ear.

'Tennent's, please,' I say, and she nods. The nod of approval. *Good choice, son. Nice vintage, that one.*

As she turns her back to find a fresh glass I look into the mirror hanging by the optics. Edged with the same floral gold design as the sign outside, the mirror looks like it belongs over a manor fireplace. *The Auld Hole in the Wall* engraved into the glass, the words scar my reflection. It's not the only thing unfamiliar about myself, though. I look different somehow. From usual, and from earlier, when I was getting ready at home. Things have changed. There's been a shift in the world. Tectonic plates have altered, creating new borders, new boundaries.

My hair looks stupid. Too adolescent for me now. I'm no longer a student – no longer a youth. After all I've been through, I'm a man now. Men need sensible haircuts. Haircuts that say 'office job' and 'loan repayment'. My face looks both too young and too old at the same time. My jaw line is squared, aggressive, masculine, but there's something childlike about the way my cheeks sit. Or is it my eyebrows? My eyes look older still, like they've seen more of life than they should have. Freeze-frames flash against the black of my pupils.

Niall, tartan and drunk
Code, swaying, frothing, steaming
I found a wee lump
Wan ae you boys pulled a blade on me

I bare my teeth – my new, shiny porcelain teeth – and turn my head slightly, examining them in the low pub lighting. I can't even remember what my old teeth looked like. Not as straight as these, probably.

I notice my hairline is different too. It's weird seeing my head from an unusual angle: it looks like someone else's, like it doesn't belong to me anymore. I trace the reflection of scars criss-crossing on the side of my head. Little bald lines carved into the haircut, like young boys with razored designs flowing above their ears. RFC dyed into their crop.

'Seen something you like?' says the barmaid, and I look back to her, to the real world.

'Sorry?'

'Taking a wee fancy to yourself?'

I laugh and she pushes the pint over to me. It leaves a slick snail-trail as it glides across the wood and I'm not sure I even want it anymore. I hand her another note and smile, my eyes flicking back to the man by the optics. He's smiling too. A new, plastic smile, with teeth he picked from a display chart.

'They range from the darker shades,' the dentist waved a hand over the standard nicotine yellows, 'up to

your celebrity white.'

'That one,' I pointed, near the middle but closer to the whites.

'Good choice,' he smiled, and I recognised the shade.

'You enjoying the music?' the barmaid asks, ignoring a man leaning heavily on the bar, waving a twenty pound note and singing along to the song. We both turn our heads towards the band.

'I am, yeah. What about you?' I say.

'Aye, not bad. Good choice of songs. I love a bit of Suede, me.'

'I know the guitarist,' I say, proud pal.

'He's good.'

I see her look over to him. Niall's standing, one foot up on his amp, nodding his head at the crowd, at the music, at himself.

'Yeah,' I say. 'Lot of potential.'

'Oh aye. Tons.'

She nods as I sip my fresh pint, her eyes tracing Niall's left hand up and down the fret board.

'Makes me wish I'd kept at it. Ah well, too late now, eh?'

'Nah,' I say, 'never too late.'

24

'So wit d'ye hink?'

'Yeah, great. I'm impressed.'

'Really?'

'Yeah, really. You guys are good. Especially considering you've only been together a few weeks.'

'Sound.'

Niall leans back in his chair, the wood creaking under his weight. He drinks deeply from his pint and looks around the pub, sweat shining on his forehead, veins popping from his neck. He nods approvingly.

'Listen, Niall, I need to tell you – Eddie's here,' I say, giving him my most serious look, eyes wide.

'Aye. And?'

'And so watch yourself.'

'Ben, I telt ye, aw ae that nonsense is finished, right? Eddie could fuckin' stand next tae me at the bar an' I'll bet ye he wouldn't even look at me, niver mind fuckin' stab me.'

'Does it not scare you though?' I say, looking around the pub, straining to find him and his mates.

'I can guarantee you, Ben, that there's tons ae folk in

here who've battered or been battered by other folk in here. It's jist how hings work, ken? This isnae EastEnders – there's nae long-runnin' feuds. This is a shitey pub in a shitey wee town. Folk get battered an' then move on wi' their lives – mibbe batter somewan else next week, mibbe no. Point is, I'm pretty sure none ae these guys are gonnae mind us bein' here.'

'How do you know all this?' I ask. 'I mean, we come from the same town, we're roughly the same age–'

'No' that roughly, auld man,' Niall interjects.

'– so how come you know so much about how things work around here? How to handle yourself?'

'How come you dinnae?' Niall sips his drink. Checkmate.

'See,' he continues, 'there's a lot that's different aboot us, Ben. We live in different parts ae town, different parents earnin' different wages, different mates tae grow up wi'. Stuff like that makes a difference, ken? So it disnae really matter that we're both kindae young, or went tae the Academy, or even that we come fae the same town. There's jist somehin different aboot me an' you. An' it's no' a bad hing, it's jist there.'

'I think you should write all of this down, Niall. All of this reflective stuff you come out with, and sell it,' I say.

'Here, that's your job, university boy.'

We both drink our beers: a mistimed moment that leaves a silence between us.

'Do you really think we're that different?' I ask, wiping my top lip.

'Aye. In some ways,' Niall replies. 'I mean, apart fae aw the stuff I've jist mentioned, I ken stuff aboot people that you seem tae huv missed. I ken how intricate social environments – such as this pub – work. But I suppose we're mibbe a wee bit similar. Sometimes. A wee bit.'

'Like how you know Shakespeare quotes?' I say.

'Aye, gonnae keep that tae yersel', Ben?' he laughs. 'But naw, at the end ae the day, we mibbe do huv different accents, different views on hings an' stuff like that, but I guess we're both jist human.'

'That's very profound of you, Niall,' I say, raising my glass.

He does the same and we clink them together with posh, aristocratic faces on.

'So, anyways, I realised I didnae ask – ken how I'm here in ma band, goin' tae college, aw ae that nonsense? Well wit the fuck huv you been up tae?'

'Well,' I begin, my voice fake-smug, 'you're not the only one who's been reading up and applying for stuff. Since having my hand brutally incapacitated and my teeth rearranged, I have been studying.'

'Studyin'?' Niall asks, setting his drink back down on the wet coaster.

'Basically, I decided – like you – that I needed out of this town, this situation. Away from all of this, basically,' I gesture around me, wrapping the whole pub and all of its patrons up in my mild disdain.

'So,' I continue, 'I read up about what other areas English graduates can go into – aside from Asda, of course – and I decided that the plan I had through uni, to become a teacher, actually wasn't all that bad. So, to cut a long story short, I sent off an application.'

'An' then wit?'

'This is the bit that hasn't gone as well for me as your plan did.'

Niall's eyebrow rises as I take another drink from my beer.

'I've not heard back yet,' I say.

'Oh,' Niall says.

There's a pause and then Niall speaks. 'Well ye niver know – they might jist huv got tons ae applications an' it's takin' them ages tae get back tae everywan.'

'I don't think so – today was the last day they said they'd get back to applicants.'

'Oh,' Niall says.

'I had it all planned out, though,' I say. 'Obviously going back to uni would've cost a lot – my parents wouldn't have been able to help me out 100% this time – but I've saved. Everything I've made through Asda I've kept in an account, and I thought this would be where it would all go, y'know? This course would be my reward for stacking all of those shelves. Except it wasn't enough.'

'How?' Niall asks.

'The cost of living in Glasgow, or even travelling through on the train would have been so high, and then I'd have needed buses to placements, food, etcetera. It all just added up and I worked out I would have been a few grand short at least.'

'Shit,' Niall says, his eyes wide at the prospect of spending that much money.

'So my dad agreed to loan me the rest. He said he couldn't cover all my costs but he could help out a bit. I'd have needed to pay him back but it would have been do-able. I'd have been able to train, get a placement, be a teacher. Except I didn't hear back.'

'So wit are ye gonnae dae now?'

I look at Niall and then back down to my drink. 'No idea. Maybe do what you did – look into a college course, start next semester, and retrain.'

'As wit?' Niall asks.

'Dunno.'

'Ben, can I tell ye somehin? That sounds, tae me, like a fuckin' stupid plan.'

'What?' I ask, snapped out of my daze, my almost-drunkeness.

'There's you givin' me aw this pish aboot followin' yer dreams, becomin' who ye really want tae be, an' now you're here talkin' aboot givin' up on yer dream efter wan wee setback.' He moves his glass out of the way and leans forward, his arms crossed on the table. 'I took a fuckin' risk, Ben. I enrolled in a college course. In Fawkirk, fuck's sake. An' now look – I'm on the course an' I'm playin' in a band. Ken why? Cause I tried. An' I tell ye – if I hadn't gotten intae Forth Valley tae dae it, I hud another college lined up efter that. An' another wan efter that. Ye dinnae jist give up, Ben. Not when yer so close. I'll ask ye this – d'ye wannae be a teacher?'

'Yeah, I do.'

'Okay. D'ye wannae stock shelves in Asda?'

'No, I don't.'

'Can ye no' see that retrainin' as sumhin else is exactly the same as stayin' at Asda, stackin' fuckin' Pot Noodles every day? Ye wouldnae be daein' wit ye want tae dae, end of. If it wis me, Ben – an' I ken we huv oor differences – but if it wis me I wouldnae settle for another Asda.'

Niall gets up and walks over to the bar. I sit there, letting his words sink in, and laugh. It's a nice change, I think, having Niall lecture me on academic ambition. He returns with two more beers, both spilling slowly down the side of the glasses and onto the carpet. I've created a monster, I think, proud of him.

'Speakin' ae Asda,' he says, sitting down and sliding a beer over to me, 'I seen Paul over at the bar there. Didnae get the chance tae speak tae him, but he nodded hello. Nice tae see he's no' still fuckin' ragin' at me, eh?'

'Maybe he can see the funny side now.' I swallow a cold mouthful down and laugh.

'Aye, I'd hope so. Oh aye, three guesses who I saw on ma first day ae college an' aw.'

'The legendary Jake and Pete?' I ask.

'The very same,' Niall says, grinning. 'On the train in. Totally heavin', like, an' they were standin' aboot three feet away fae me. Both in their Asda uniforms.'

'Really? They took the transfer?' I say, remembering that glorious phone call where I embraced unemployment once more, and said 'I would like to politely decline the offer of a transfer and would, as such, be terminating my period of employment with Asda.'

'Must have. So there's the two ae them, standin' chattin', both total dour-faced cunts, an' I decide I'd really like tae hear wit they're bein' so serious aboot.'

'You didn't...' I begin.

'I fuckin' did. So up I gits, oot ae ma nice comfy seat, an' I squeeze past aw these people 'til I'm only a couple ae folk away fae them. They dinnae notice, an' jist keep on chattin' away.'

'What were they saying?' I ask.

'Ken wit wis so serious? Wit wis so brutal it wis gettin' them doon on such a nice wee mornin'?'

Niall sips his pint, relishing the suspense. Maybe he should train to be a storyteller, I think, relaying old Scots tales to American tourists.

'Some new manager at Fawkirk Asda,' Niall continues, 'wis huvin' a crackdoon on shabby uniforms an' they'd both been disciplined fur the state ae their trousers.'

'Is that it?' I ask, a smile teasing at the edges of my lips.

'That wis wit wis so important tae the two ae them. Fuck's sake, can ye imagine?'

'Bear in mind,' I point out, 'that no kind of disciplining would ever get you down, Niall. You'd just tell them to fuck off and throw food everywhere.'

Niall laughs, shaking his head at the memory.

'Aye well, stupid fuckin' job, takin' itself too seriously

anyway. Christ, I mean, at the end ae the day, it's only a sales job, ken? I'm no' runnin' RBS or anyhin.'

'Probably for the best,' I wink, and Niall laughs. 'So what happened then? Pretty awkward being on the same train. You sure they didn't see you?'

'Oh aye, there's mair tae the story. So I'm listenin' tae them gabbin' on aboot this shitey manager an' some dick comes along wantin' tae get past. An' everywan has tae squeeze in an' move aboot until they get through. So efter this cunt's gone I breathe oot, stand back in ma spot, but they've moved closer. The folk inbetween us huv moved tae another wee space an' I'm left standin' right next tae them.'

'Did they notice then?' I ask.

'Too fuckin' right they noticed. Turned their backs on me straight away, sly as fuck, like. Spent the whole rest ae the journey like that, whisperin' as quietly as they could. So I pull oot ma mp3 player, stick on a wee bit ae The Corries. I turn it up right loud, ken? So everywan on the carriage can hear *Ye Jacobites By Name* blastin' oot. Hope that pissed them off.'

Niall laughs and I imagine him there, on the Edinburgh-Dunblane train, in full Highland regalia, beating a bodhrán to a steady pulse while Jake and Pete stand, backs turned, grinding their teeth.

'Always hated The Corries, they dicks. Said it wis 'shite old folk music'. I tried tellin' them, even played em *Scots Wha Hae*, ken? They laughed, said it wis aboot as relevant tae Scotland as they wee tartan shops on the

Royal Mile, y'know? An' I telt them, in nae uncertain terms, that they could away an' fuck themselves. The Corries are aboot rememberin' the past, no' celebratin' it, an' lookin' tae the future. Bein aware ae the Scotland behind ye while ye look at the Scotland ahead. Nuthin' wrong wi' identifying wi' yer ain culture, fuck's sake.'

He drinks deeply, quelling the anger in his belly with more cold, frothy beer. I begin to wonder where tonight is leading for Niall. Certainly, if it was me I'd be cutting loose, but I remember how Niall was the last time he went out on the brew.

'Anyways,' he continues, stretching out the first syllable, 'the whole way there I'm pissin' aff these two fannies an' eventually I hear Jake go 'Fuck's sake, what a loser' as the doors opened at Fawkirk. Man, I didnae ken whether tae laugh or cry. Me, a fuckin' loser? I got aff the train an' jist stood there, kindae dazed by wit he jist said, kindae angry an' aw, an' then I thought 'Fuck it, I'm gonnae be late fur college' an' that wis that. End of.'

"What a loser' – classic!' I say. 'You know how you were saying Eddie won't touch us now, because it's all over, unless we do something ... D'you think the same is true for them?'

'Aye,' Niall says, nodding. 'The only difference is, they two are more likely tae dae sumhin.'

I glance round and see Eddie and Chloe at the bar. His arm is looped over her shoulders, pulling her close to the side of his chest. I think about how much I risked just to be that guy – the one with his arm around her – and then

I remember, I wasn't ever going to be that guy. That was the point.

Shaking the thought from my head, I point to Niall's glass, now nearly empty again.

'Another beer for the rock star?'

'Aye, why no'?' Niall says, grinning that familiar grin that says 'This is fucking amazing. I am so wasted.'

I get up and walk towards the bar, concentrating on my balance and not knocking anyone else over, but by the time I've ordered the drinks I hear Niall calling over. I look round and he's pointing towards the drum kit and miming a guitar. I give him the thumbs up. Gotcha.

The barmaid passes the two pints over towards me and gives me that 'We're on the same page, me and you' nod before I walk back to the table.

'Eh, this one's a bit of a mellow one, if yous don't mind?' says Ann, as the band takes their places. Niall with an acoustic guitar now, Charlie using brushes on his kit.

'It's about Scotland,' she continues, 'and about home. It's called *Caledonia*.'

Niall strums out the chords and I weave through the crowd, back to my seat, through groups with linked arms and drinks held high.

There's a different vibe sitting down here. The table is round the corner from the band so the sound is different, obviously, and they're playing a quiet number, but it's something more than that. A calmness of sorts. I sit peacefully, my eyes unfocused, but intently listening to the band; Niall's gentle guitar work, Charlie's soft backing on the drums, Lauren's slow bass, and Ann's voice, high above the crowd.

It feels nice; this warm, drunk feeling, with Niall's words still sitting inside my head.

Ye dinnae jist give up, Ben. Not when yer so close.

if it wis me I wouldnae settle for another Asda

My phone beeps, bringing me back from my little daydream. The handset is still unfamiliar and it takes me a while to access the message.

Letter for you. Dad.

I text back.

At night?

Signed for. Missed it this morning.
Red card through the door.
Picked it up on way back from work.

Ah, thanks.
Just leave it on the hall table.
I'll be in late – got my house key.
Night.

From some Glasgow Uni.

I stare at the text. The pub is silent now – I can't hear anything from the crowds or the band. Just imagining Dad's voice in my head.

From some Glasgow Uni.

I stare at the text and then at the two fresh pints sitting in front of me.

From some Glasgow Uni.

Ye dinnae jist give up, Ben. Not when yer so close.

And then I run.

The pub doors swing shut behind me and I have to push the bouncer out of my way.

'Oi!' he shouts, every cartoon, shaven-headed inch of him already teeming with adrenaline, ready for a fight.

I turn right and run past the kilt shop, then left past the old court. The first murder by gunshot happened right here, Niall once told me. But things like that don't matter anymore. Not history. Not the past. Nothing matters, except that letter and what it might say. What it might mean.

I take the concrete steps two at a time, climbing up to the back alleys and then up on to Royal Terrace. I run up, over the canal bridge, my lungs burning, my legs cramping. I spit, trying to rid the stale taste of beer from my mouth, but the saliva gets caught by the wind and splatters my shirt. My skin starts to prickle with sweat. Warm from my body, but cold against the wind as it blows down my shirt collar. I feel clammy, sickly. My mind flicks to the hangover after that night at Chloe's flat, when the concussion subsided and left me feeling flu-like.

Forwards, I charge my legs. Like horses riding into battle I will them on. I'm one street away from home, from that letter. I think about what it might say, my heart pumping harder and harder, forcing blood and beer around my body until my head's spinning at the prospect of a 'Yes'. My stomach churns as I think 'No' and I have to will the alcohol back down. My throat burns as I retch and spit again. Nothing matters. Not history. Not the past.

I'm nearly there.

My legs fail as I run up the street and I'm reduced to

a limp, my hands clutching my side, feeling the burning sting of lactic acid course through my abdomen. I breathe heavily, each lungful whooshing in and out of my mouth like a steam engine slowing at a station.

And then I'm home.

I push the door open, still limping, and see it sitting next to the art-deco lamp Mum bought from a car boot sale.

Square and white, this letter could change my life.

I check the addressee. This is really it. My name, big and bold.

BEN HAMILTON

The flap on the back of the envelope is stuck firm so I tear the side open, exposing the edges of the letter inside. My heart is hammering in my chest and I close my eyes for a moment. I breathe in the fresh papery smell, letting it overwhelm the stale beer in my mouth and the sweat under my shirt, and then pull the letter out. My fingertips tingle under the paper and I let the envelope drop to the ground, the front door still swinging open in the breeze. The air catches the torn paper and takes it up and away as I try to make sense of the letter.

As the breeze dies down, the door swings shut. I look up to see my both of parents standing at the other end of the hall, wine glasses in hand, a low TV soundtrack in the background. My mum says 'Well?' and I clear my throat.

'I'm in.'